I0788097

This Is How We Love

The Foto-Novel

Original edition April 1995
Revised edition March 2025

A History of *This Is How We Love*

SPECIAL ESSAY FOR THE 30TH-ANNIVERSARY OF THE TIE-IN BOOK EDITION

By Gretchen Millnar

WHERE TO BEGIN? With the fabled "curse" that afflicted nearly everyone associated with this notorious film, including the gaffers and all three lighting technicians, not to mention the poor thespian pooch, Charlie Boy, the first of two canines to play "Bones the Blind Dog"? Or should we begin with the scheduled three-week shoot that ballooned into a 16-month odyssey after myriad issues, including sickness (dengue fever from mosquitoes that hitched a ride in a spray bottle specially imported from Venezuela by the lead stylist), a Category 4 hurricane (the first believed to have occurred in California since the previous one tore through mastodons 2.5 million years ago), an unplanned explosion inside a porta-potty (as opposed to all of those *planned* explosions inside porta-potties), multiple babies conceived (and then delivered) on set, and, yes, a helicopter crash that took out an ammo depot (instantly detonating $186 million in Tomahawk cruise missiles, not counting the five that inadvertently launched and had to be shot down before penetrating Canadian airspace)? Or how about the strange fact that even though *This Is How We Love* amazingly, astonishingly, incredibly managed to (reportedly) win a best-picture Academy Award, no legal copies of the film are now available, minus a few VHS bootleg editions one can purchase only after diving deep into the moist, dark bowels of eBay?

The movie's backstory is undoubtedly already infamous among a certain type of fandom, the type to have memorized every line in *The Warriors* or the kind to have managed to obtain the ultra-rare outtakes of *Back to the Future* starring Eric Stoltz *before* they surfaced on YouTube, and before they were quickly removed. But for those with an actual life, which I'm assuming and hoping you are currently living, allow me to provide a bit of non-essential cinematic history.

It's 1990, and a small-time television writer with a murky past, Matthew Michaud, 46, is looking to branch out from the lesser realm of TV scribe and into the loftier principalities of the silver screen. With eight episodes of *The Rockford Files* under his double-pronged, leather belt—as well as a made-for-TV movie starring Christopher Knight of *Brady Bunch* fame (1984's *Rocks Along the Horizon*, CBS)—Michaud's dream was to bring his somewhat limited skill set to theaters, a dream he had nurtured since piloting his 1971 V-8 Buick Electra from Cleveland, Ohio, straight to Hollywood in the fuggy summer of 1975.

Michaud, if nothing else, was a believer in his God-given right to an audience, in his entitlement as a natural-born American citizen to elevate the ideas he scribbled down on his legal pad at a Sunset Boulevard Denny's onto the big screen and to then have them transmitted across the world. But this didn't hold true only for writing. Michaud was most keen to *direct,* to become a true auteur, much like his cinematic heroes, the writers-directors Éric Rohmer, Ingmar Bergman, and John Huston.

One of Michaud's most treasured script ideas was for an epic, hours-long drama, to take place in the current day (the then current mid-1990s), featuring at least 20 disparate characters, with endlessly intertwining plotlines striated throughout the film like the fatty veins in a high-end rib eye.

The resulting 570-page, handwritten script that Michaud worked on in that Hollywood Denny's no longer exists *in toto* . . . but fragments can now easily be found if you pay a visit to the archives at the Harry Ransom Center, at the University of Texas at Austin.

The original title, *Heartshaped Moonshadows,* soon morphed into *How We Love,* which mutated into *This Is Everything,* which became *The Way Love Has to Be,* which was simplified into *Love,* which was re-written as *This Is Love,* which transformed into *This Crazy Thing Called Life,* only to then be re-styled as *This Is Life with Regular American People,* which became *Night Comes Down,* which was overhauled as *Smash* and then *American Berserk* and then finally—after sticking a not-so-smooth landing, years later—to the title we're familiar with today: *This Is How We Love.*

With the lodestar of a sufficient title now firmly entrenched into the stratosphere of his starscape, Michaud set about editing down the mammoth script, beginning in May 1990, with the aid of a 1962 white Olympia typewriter gifted to him by his mother back in Ohio. Across the ribbon-spool cover, in red ink and in cursive, was written: *This Machine Kills Audiences.* Toiling away for five months within his one-bedroom Mid-City rental, Michaud chiseled and chopped his miracle screenplay down to a lean, 346-page script, all the while remaining true and plumb to his original intentions.

Which is not to say that the movie's new, streamlined plots were in any way simple.

No.

If you're prone to motion sickness, now might be the time to grab a rail or even a bucket. Either way, here we go:

It's 1993, and former astronaut Bizz Adams, 54, lives in a "just your average" 5,000-square-foot mansion, within a compound, within Everytown, U.S.A.—Brentwood, Los Angeles. Haunted by a mishap in space that he fears he could have been responsible for (lighting a celebratory cigar in an oxygen-rich environment), Bizz remains preoccupied with a past that he can't control and a future with, seemingly, very little excitement or possibility. His middle-aged wife, Azure Adams—longing for all the advantages and perks once associated with her proximity to fame—has pickled her lethargy in gin-and-tonics, and her sexual release in the backyard shed with the compound's Mexican-American gardener, Ray Ray. Bizz the Former Astronaut and Azure the Cheating Alcoholic have two adult children: Bobby (a former NASCAR driver with a burned face) and Melissa (a troubled twentysomething who suffers from depression and a stuttering habit). Making matters even more complicated (remember, this was the 90s) is the fact that Melissa is, gulp, a "lesbian" who volunteers at a suicide hotline a few evenings a week, and yet her biggest dream is to teach disadvantaged, inner-city middle-schoolers advanced algebra.

Still with me?

The wife of Bobby the Former NASCAR Driver, Rachey, works as an escort to help her husband afford the cosmetic surgery for his scarred face so that he might one day work as a dashing, exclusive real-estate agent in the Brentwood, Los Angeles, area. But there remains a void in Bobby and Rachey's marriage, one they attempt to fill by taking the unusual step of adopting a fully-grown Native-American with an intellectual disability. The man's name is Pecker, short for "Peckerwood." His parents, we come to learn, have died in a forest fire due to the unhinged greed of a consortium of white, wealthy real-estate developers. Tragic. All of it.

Bobby's eldest son, Timmy, is a world-famous "rock-and-roll songwriter" who specializes in this new wild sound called "grunge." One problem: he is on illegal drugs. But there is hope! Flatterhy, the deaf and youngest child of Bobby, wants nothing more than to hear music for the first time in his life. More specifically, he wants to hear a Grunge Song written by his older, rock-and-roller brother, Timmy. Might this just be the inspiration needed for Timmy to escape the druggy noose coiled so tightly around his neck?

Just beyond this beribboned jumble of untidy plot spikings exists a mysterious homeless man, Klat, who has taken up residence outside the Adams family's gated compound, on a cabana-striped beach towel at the bottom of the long, winding driveway. Who is this mysterious shoeless character? And how could he have *possibly* ended up here? Could the rumors be true that he was once a *millionaire?* Why yes, those rumors are indeed true! For he was once a helicopter pilot in South Africa, adorned with a very particular skill set that now might just help Bobby in his quest to sell Brentwood houses! That is, if Bobby can afford the pricey facial surgery performed by a . . . *female* surgeon.

Sprinkled into this flat, two-dimensional gumbo are the following uninspiring creations: George the Black Gangbanger who befriends Bizz the Former Astronaut after a car accident, which involves a Bentley that can make only right turns; Matthew Schwartzmann, the gay son of the Jewish, "ethnic" neighbor, Arnold Schwartzmann; Bobby's sister, Maraket, the owner of a well-regarded luxury-soap emporium in Beverly Hills; N.F.L. quarterback Robbie Hostetleir of the Denver Broncos (seriously), who, in his one and only scene, provokes a fight at a community college's dance club; the aforementioned Bones the Blind Dog, who can see "better" than any full-sighted human; a middle-school vice principal named Kirsty Mallano, who is "tough and fair but a lesbian" and in love with Melissa; Melissa's live-and-let-live swing-dancing roommate with a clubfoot, Vicky; Topper, Vicky's scraggly, Gen X boyfriend, who works as a skateboarding-and-blading messenger, and who has accidentally stumbled upon a secret, powerful legal document that could very well threaten the world's rainforests; and Manuel, the schizophrenic, brilliant son of Ray Ray the Gardener and Angel the Cook, who befriends three young men at the local community college—Tony, Harold, and Victor—who, in reality, are but mere figments of Manuel's troubled imagination (all three played, incidentally, by the writer-director himself, Matthew Michaud); and so much less.

Okay, are you *still* still with me?

Once the script was written to Michaud's exacting, unique specifications, it was time for this eager auteur to obtain production funding—no easy task in the best of circumstances, a task made that much more difficult due to the early-1990s recession and the near-impossible challenge of convincing a producer to hand over $10 million to a first-time director who was best known for a few written (and often re-written) adventures of Jim Rockford, the middle-aged, trailer-dwelling P.I. down by the Malibu shore, as well an unproduced, X-rated animated film called *Tubes and Circles*.

And guess what? Hollywood passed en masse. Paramount was a hard no. As was Warner Bros., Disney, and Miramax. (Remember Miramax?) Within short order, Twentieth Century Fox passed, as well as Universal, Columbia, and ten lesser studios.

Apparently, a now streamlined 246-page script, with 20-plus characters and as many plots and subplots, wasn't quite considered the "get" Michaud desperately needed it to be. So he was back where he started, another hack in a diner jotting down ideas nobody particularly liked and certainly wasn't willing to pay for. Another Hollywood swing; another Hollywood miss.

Until it wasn't.

What comes next is a bit muddied, as all stories tend to be when they involve—even tenuously—the Mob. Contrary to perceived belief, the Mafia is very much an "equal opportunity" organization when it comes to funding movies. Yes, gangsters invest heavily in pornography, and chances are if you saw an on-screen orgasm in the 80s or 90s, it was heavily subsidized by La Cosa Nostra.

But throughout the years, going back to at least the mid-1930s, the Mob has funded hundreds of films, across *all* genres, some of which might even have won an Academy Award or two.

Which brings us to *This Is How We Love*.

The following information comes from Matthew Michaud's 2004 memoir, *Winning at Hollywood*. Although self-published, a few used xeroxed copies can still be found on AbeBooks or Amazon, and they tend to fetch upward of $2,500 or more. If you see one cheaper, grab it.

So . . . it's March 1991, and, armed with a fresh script and a dream that refuses to die, Michaud reaches out to a friend of a friend, a criminal from Cleveland nicknamed The Rabbit. Michaud copies the script at a "copy center" (remember, this is pre-email), packages it, and delivers it via the U.S. Postal Service. Within the week, Michaud receives back word:

The Rabbit, it seems, absolutely loves the characters, adores the myriad plots, and is just tickled by the way the movie does things "no one else has ever done before." Yes, The Rabbit has previously invested in a few "pornographical" films but it was now time for him to "move on to a more reputable realm, to more reputable projects without all the jizz, unless the story calls for it."

"I was ecstatic," Michaud writes in *Winning at Hollywood*. "This was the break I had been waiting so many years for oh yeah! Sometimes all a great idea needs is a champion, and I found him in Rabbit and his various associates."

With the money in hand, Michaud immediately set to work hiring his crew, most of whom he had worked with back in the *Rockford Files* days. He also hired a casting director he admired who had worked on a few of his favorite films, including *The French Connection* and *Lenny,* the Dustin Hoffman biopic about the life and drug-fueled death of 1960s comedian Lenny Bruce.

What happens next is, perhaps, not so entirely surprising.

As Melanie Losos explained in her 1997 *Premiere* magazine piece on *This Is How We Love:* "The Rabbit, no fan of 'traditional' casting choices, chose another route: to hire actors and actresses who he, himself, respected for their looks, their ability to express sufficient emotions on the big screen, and—most importantly—their willingness to pay him for the opportunity to do so."

Put simply: The Rabbit sought to hire actors who had the necessary amount of cash to fork over to become a star—on a sliding scale directly related to the amount of speaking lines they would have in the movie. Fame was at the ready for anyone . . . as long as they had the money.

You have the money? Congratulations, you just got your big break!

To say that a cast of unknowns stepped forward for this opportunity would do a disservice to your typical "cast of unknowns." As *Premiere* put it: "Not quite 100 people reached out to The Rabbit by way of advertisements strategically taped to light poles in L.A.'s more upscale neighborhoods, seeded in the dressing rooms of high-end boutiques, and littering the V.I.P. lounges of gentlemen's clubs in close proximity to airports. The auditioning for the movie involved zero acting and absolutely no improvisation, just a detailed, very precise audit of a prospective performer's bank account by Rabbit's 'eagle-eyed Hebrew.'"

A cast of more than twenty actors/benefactors (and one lucky pooch whose owner desperately wanted the world to fall in love with his golden retriever–husky mix) was now shakily in place.

And yet, something must have felt off for Michaud because he did what so few artists would have done in his situation: rather than make a film poorly, or even illicitly, with a cast of amateurs, he thought better of it . . . and returned the entire amount of cash to The Rabbit. He then (perhaps out of a deep wish to not be shot surreptitiously) gifted The Rabbit "a few thousand for his troubles."

Within weeks, however, Michaud had walked straight into another bizarre situation that allowed him to make his ambitious film—this time *without* any input from the Mafia.

Michaud was spending his aimless days pacing up and down Sunset Boulevard, as well as listlessly paging through the trades. That's when, in March 1991, he saw a small ad in the back of an issue of *Variety:*

FINANCIALLY SECURE BUSINESSMAN
Looking to Break Into Movies!
Searching for teh [sic] Right Project
(Little to no raunch, please!)
Contact Here:
PO Box 38209
Poolesville Maryland 20822

For this story, let's jump back a few years . . .

It's the fall of 1984, and a 67-year-old Maryland former industrial-refrigerator mechanic named James Calder Walton has fashioned, as a lark and for his sole granddaughter, an adorable stuffed dog with floppy ears and a wide smile. He names his toy "The Pound Poochy Pooch," after a beloved childhood dog, and then sells, in 1984, his entire line to Tonka. Yes, The Pound Poochy Pooches becomes "Pound Puppies." And Walton is now a multi-millionaire.

Just your typical success story. But behind all the money and fame, Walton's biggest aspiration happened to coincide with a very American one: to somehow find a way into producing big-budget Hollywood movies.

Which is why he placed that small, enticing ad in the back of *Variety* in March 1991.

"I contacted him immediately," wrote Michaud in *Winning at Hollywood.* "I'm not sure how, but I felt a strong creative, almost spiritual, connection with this man in Maryland. I knew that whoever opened that P.O. Box was going to finance my movie without money earned through loansharking and brutal violence. That was my hope, anyway."

A script of *This Is How We Love* was immediately FedExed to Walton, who, according to Michaud, absolutely adored it: "[He] said it was the best script he ever read. And he told me he read lots! And this was a guy who's favorite movie was *Terms of Endearment!*"

But Walton did have one stipulation, and it was a major one: That he, and he alone, would be allowed to choose the actors and actresses to play the film's characters.

Yes, the script, the direction, and any and all creative decisions would be left to Michaud. But when it came to choosing the stars and co-stars of the film, Walton would have the first and last word. He had a vision, and that vision involved various friends and family members he felt would be absolutely perfect for this project.

Facing the choice of having this Washington, D.C., businessman cast the movie, or not making the movie at all, Michaud chose the former. There really wasn't a viable alternative. The movie needed to be made. And, to be fair, Walton was not charging the actors for the opportunity. He was no con man; he was no criminal.

Walton belonged to the United Methodist Church in Potomac, Maryland, as well as to its Dramatic and Music Club, which had in recent years put on such productions as *Joseph and the Amazing Technicolor Dreamcoat, Godspell, Jesus Christ Superstar,* and a heavily reimagined version of *Fiddler on the Roof,* which had nixed the overtly Jewish element. From these stagings—in 1986, 1987, 1988, and 1989—came the core group of actors to later star in *This Is How We Love.*

Here are but a few:

MAX PEARSON—"Bizz Adams, Former Astronaut"—47, orthodontist, husband and
father, Pontius Pilate in the United Methodist's production of *Jesus Christ Superstar*

GLENN PRICE—"Klat the Wise Homeless Man"—46, real-estate developer,
husband and father, sarcastic rainbow-Afroed disciple in *Godspell*

SHANNON FERGUSON—"Azure Adams, Wife of Bizz Adams, Alcoholic"—44, homemaker,
mother of three, shy and bespectacled whore in *Joseph and the Amazing Technicolor Dreamcoat . . .*

Etc.

With this crack cast in place, it was now time to shoot the movie!

On the morning of June 4, 1992—and scheduled for only three weeks, with all 125 scenes to be shot in sequence—the production began in the Brentwood neighborhood of Los Angeles, with cast and crew staying at a nearby Westin hotel. From here, let's take a glance at the diary that Michaud kept, and later published, in its entirety, in his self-published memoir.

It begins with such limitless possibility:

"Crew and cast bused to location—excitement all around! Table read goes spectacular. Six hours. Will probably
need to cut down. Everyone getting along famously. Then over to the crafts table for fresh delicious seafood! Back
tomorrow at dawn to begin!"   —JUNE 4, 1992

"A bit more nausea among the cast and crew than I expected. Hoping this is just a normal and temporary part of
the movie-making process! The jitters!"   —JUNE 5, 1992

"Food poisoning running rampant. Half off oysters might have been the culprit. Fired craft services director. Noticed filthy fingernails when he gave me the finger, also 'COCK LORD' knuckle tattoos. Confirm CV next time!"

—JUNE 6, 1992

"Lighting technician Mitch burned to death in a somewhat unfortunate incident. Two gaffers also burned to death in another somewhat unlucky accident. Craft services tent better today! Promising efforts to keep food at sanitary temperature! Isn't that wonderful?!"

—JUNE 7, 1992

"Charlie Boy the pooch escaped pen and bounded onto 405, narrowly avoiding 18 wheeler! Lucky! But then flattened by 914 Porsche helmed by actress from *Boy Meets World*. But hey! Will at least make the news!"

—JUNE 9, 1992

"Actress Shannon refusing to say: 'I hate Hispanics.' Fails to understand that saying 'I hate Hispanics' would make the world *better* for Hispanics! So we compromised. She'll now say: 'I hate Histamines.' To be dubbed over with 'I hate Hispanics' in post. None the wiser!"

—JUNE 13, 1992

"Second lightning technician killed by lightning strike. Spinach quiche was particularly delicious in food tent! Learned yours truly has a nickname on set: 'PAG.' For "Pussy Assed Goblin." Betting everyone has a fun name like that!"

—JUNE 15, 1992

"There goes the last of the lighting technicians and that remaining gaffer! Desserts positively delish!" —JUNE 17, 1992

The shoot, of course, blows right past its three-week planned schedule and enters into a new phase, only to then face even more breakdowns, diseases, and, yes, horrible/violent deaths:

"Category 4 hurricane! Mud cleared just in time for outbreak of dengue fever moving rapidly through cast. Everyone lives! But for that one worker with the oversized forehead who speaks into walkie-talkie and smells vaguely of maple syrup. Still don't know what he did or if he even belonged on set!"   —OCTOBER 1, 1992

"Beginning to think shoot is 'cursed.' Port-A-Potty explodes! Stunt coordinator dies while taking shit. Don't know why. Maybe just one of those mysteries never to be solved!"   —NOVEMBER 2, 1992

"Solved: dynamite sticks placed beneath Port-A-Potty. But who put them there? And why?! Who knows! Maybe just one of those mysteries never to be solved!"   —NOVEMBER 8, 1992

"Solved! New chef put the dynamite sticks in the Port-A-Potty. But why?! Maybe just one of those mysteries never to be solved?!!"   —DECEMBER 9, 1992

"Solved! New chef is mentally unhinged! But absolute wizard with souffles! *Triple* check CV next time!"   —DECEMBER 11, 1992

And then there were the on-set relationships. As Robert Johanssen wrote in his 1997 *GQ* piece on *This Is How We Love*: "Groins were most certainly clinked."

More now from Michaud's diary:

"Jimbo fucking Luisa who's fucking Glen fucking Charley who['s] fucking Luisa who's screwing Erica fucking the intern banging Glenn fucking with Jimbo screwing Erica! Yours truly may be the only one not sleeping with anyone! By design, of course. I could snap my fingers and turn this set into my own personal *Playboy* grotto . . . but I've got a movie to make! *Art!*"   —MARCH 7, 1993

"First on-set baby born. Heard wag say 'So this is how they love!' Couldn't help but giggle!"   —MARCH 10, 1993

"6th baby born on set. I am praying that this doesn't push back film! You know what Geena Davis and Susan Sarandon have in common? Not having a fucking baby while fucking shooting Thelma and Louise!!!"
                                                                                              —MARCH 14, 1993

"Even the new dog gives birth! Not a *male* after all! Anybody *not* fucking around here? Tired of this shit! Want *my* movie! American *needs* my movie!"   —MARCH 25, 1993

All that seemed to matter, clearly, to this auteur was that he finish his film on time and on budget, and woe to anyone who stood in his way.

No one was about to stop him!

Except, that is, for one man.

The difficult relationship between Michaud and his leading actor/Maryland orthodontist, Dr. Max Pearson, has been discussed at length in magazine articles and in books, including *Wolves Outside the Pack: 1990s Films and the Legacies They Left Behind* (Penguin/Random House, 2001)*,* but never with any input from Pearson *himself,* who, over the years, has refused numerous interviews.

And yet . . . Dr. Pearson *did* accept my invitation in June 2022 to talk because "what's in the past is in the past, at last."

I asked Dr. Pearson the following: *Were all of the stories about the fights on set exaggerated? Or were they as intense as has been reported?*

His answer:

"No, in fact, if anything, they were even *worse* than what's been reported. There was a real fear the movie would never get made at all. We fought on the set constantly. *Always.* Over everything. If I made an expression of disgust, he wanted one of pleasure. I'd pet the dog and [the] dog would look up at me. I would yell 'Cut' and [Michaud] would yell that only *he* was the one who was allowed to yell 'Cut.' But the dog was supposed to be *blind!* And he's *looking* up at me! I didn't even know what it was called, but I liked to stay in character entirely throughout the shoot, with no breaks. Michaud would ask me a question and [I'd] answer as an aging astronaut and not as a very successful Maryland orthodontist. That drove him *nuts!*"

Were there any actual physical fights?
  "The fight everyone knows about—or one of the fights—is after the helicopter crashed into the army depot, blowing up the Tomahawk missiles. It was a stunt with a real helicopter but not a real pilot. He was just someone Michaud knew who claimed to fly in Vietnam. But he couldn't fly anything. I was almost beheaded. Michaud laughed. We came to blows more than a few times. I look back and understand both our positions. It was always my dream to act. This was his big shot. We had different styles. We both wanted the film to be wonderful. My only regret is that I turned down the sex scene with the woman playing my wife [Shannon Ferguson]. I knew her from church. But no matter how many times I promised to wear a beige 'Penis Pouch' over my genitals, my real-life wife balked."

What was your relationship with Michaud like in later years? Did you ever speak again?
  "We never did. He did his thing, I did mine. I never wished him harm, and I think he felt the same. But we never did talk again. In his strange way, he was brilliant. But he never could overcome his wrong beginnings."

It's worth noting that so little is known about Michaud's life after 1994 that one can almost forget that so little is known about his life *before* 1994. Yes, Michaud wrote for various television shows, including *The Rockford Files.* But what about his childhood? And his young adulthood? Where did he come from? How did he end up where he ended up?
  We know he was born in Annapolis, Maryland, in 1944, to a career naval officer and a stay-at-home mother. We also know he had a slight stutter and a nervous energy one teacher described, in a 2001 interview, as "the most irritating personality trait I have ever seen in a six-year-old that didn't involve flinging [excreta]."

More details trickle in as Michaud grows older. Shunning college, an 18-year-old Michaud took a bus, in February 1964, to the lone city outside Annapolis he was familiar with, his mother's hometown of Cleveland, Ohio. He immediately launched an import-export wig company that he called MegaStar #1 European Hair Inter-Continental. The rationale for this particular business choice remains hidden. Within 18 months, and after a few lawsuits over slight scalp charring caused by the "proprietary synthetic" used in the wigs, Michaud moved on to his next business venture: a boutique advertising agency that specialized in "humorous" radio ads for local businesses. Humor is always effective in advertising. Except when your main client happens to be the local hospice.

Michaud's third business venture seems to have taken place within the freshly built Parmatown Indoor Mall, a store devoted to two of the hottest trends at the time: minidresses and melted fondue cheeses.

That store lasted six months.

From this point forward, very little is known about Michaud until his eventual arrival in Hollywood, in the summer of 1975—or *had* been known.

On a hunch, I decided to travel to Cleveland to search more deeply into the public records stored in city hall, as well as within the genealogical files at the town historical center and in the microfiche files at the *Cleveland Plain Dealer* newspaper archives. I stayed for three weeks. And what I found has never before been reported, or even alluded to, in any book or magazine article. And it is thus:

Matthew Michaud—the infamous auteur of one of the worst movies to have ever won a best Academy Award, owner of a last name that has since become a Hollywood verb (he "Michauded that film")—escaped from Cleveland to Hollywood not to "make it" but . . . to "escape it."

Furthermore, Matthew Michaud was affiliated with the Cleveland Mob—perhaps not as an "official" member, yet . . . someone who was most definitely "linked."

I do not write this lightly. As my legal adviser has pointed out numerous times over the past few months: "You better be right about this, my girl!"

I feel that I am.

Think back to earlier in this essay. Do you remember Michaud reaching out to a friend of a friend named The Rabbit back in Cleveland? And do you remember how The Rabbit was willing to produce Michaud's dream movie project but only by charging actors and actresses for the opportunity to star in it?

Well, let's take a closer look at that.

To begin, The Rabbit and Michaud were not strangers.

The Rabbit and Michaud were, in reality, best friends, and had been since they met as 19-year-olds in Cleveland, shortly after Michaud arrived in February 1964.

More than that, Michaud and The Rabbit had been involved in many ill-advised, illegal schemes; and the businesses that Michaud supposedly owned were merely cover stories to protect Mob-related schemes for tax purposes.

Michaud had a more artistic temperament than his friend, The Rabbit. But he was anything but an innocent.

This is what I discovered in my research:

In the fall of 1967, The Rabbit (real name: Stefan Trigiano) was arrested for a scam that left half a dozen Marines on shore leave penniless, nude, and locked in a Gino's Fried Chicken lavatory. Michaud, broke and unemployed, willingly took the fall and did seven years in the Cleveland House of Corrections in exchange for a healthy lump sum that he ultimately planned to use however he saw fit.

But getting out of jail didn't quite set him straight. Soon after his release, he headed directly out to L.A., where Rabbit had already fled after allegedly impregnating the wife, mistress, and daughter of the Cleveland Mafia's brutal underboss, Marty "Li'l Cheeks" Battiatta. And while Michaud did write for TV, his primary source of income was (with help from his good pal, Rabbit) conning Hollywood wannabes, rubes, and frauds.

There were at least six scams conducted, in tandem, by The Rabbit and Michaud, one involving the opportunity to participate in a 1983 porn parody called *On Hairy Pond.*

When it comes to *This Is How We Love,* however, a funny thing happened on the way to the average Mob-Related Hollywood Swindle:

At the age of 40—perhaps sensing that he was close to, or even directly at, the midway point between birth and demise—Matthew Michaud stepped back and seemingly took a closer look at both himself and the 346-page script he had written.

In the case of the latter, he liked what he saw.

In the case of the former, seemingly not so much.

It was time to go straight.

Perhaps he was worthy of creative pursuits, after all. Lord knows he was surrounded by thousands of lesser Hollywood talents who seemed to be doing quite well for themselves!

Perhaps Michaud *did* have a purpose here on Earth, one without the risk of another seven-year stretch in the pokey.

So when he answered James Calder Walton's ad in the back of *Variety,* in March 1991, it was not for nefarious purposes but for truly artistic ones: Michaud desperately wanted to make his dream project and he wanted to do so legally.

Yes, he'd have to work with semi- and non-professional actors and congregants from a Methodist church in Maryland . . . but at least the project would happen! The right way.

With the newly infused money from Walton, Michaud was all set to entertain viewers with a cinematic vision that would break boundaries and pave the way for a future generation of filmmakers!

In fact, there was now so much money invested that there would be even more opportunity for Michaud to realize his dream! More characters! More unnecessary plots! Not just a blind dog . . . but a deaf man! A mysterious but wise homeless man who turns out to be a millioniaire! A subplot involving this new musical sensation "Grunge"! A classful of urban Black characters who are brilliant at advanced algebra! A white teacher to lead them! A gay character! Actually, a smattering of gay characters!

Michaud rehired the production crew he had worked with on *The Rockford Files,* as well as the casting director he had admired from *The French Connection* and *Lenny.*

And he began shooting.

And shooting.

And shooting.

And shooting . . .

Sixteen months later, on September 11, 1993, it was at last a wrap.

And then the editing began: 263 hours of footage, edited down to 110 hours, then down to 67 hours (after dispensing with several subplots, one involving a multi-species party on the Moon), whittled to a tight 37 hours (excising a subplot about an explorer discovering an ancient Egyptian tablet that solves the world's most difficult algebra equation), sliced even further down to 23 hours, and then to 15 hours. Finally, after dispensing with yet another subplot, this one involving the parents of the skateboarding-and-blading messenger—specifically his father, who ritually sacrifices his penis to save his life among hostile South American tribesmen—we arrive at the final running time of 3 hours and 48 minutes (not counting the credits).

With the movie at last complete, a date was set for this lengthy opus to open wide to the public.

Which it proceeded to do on April 19, 1994.

In precisely one theater, at the AMC Six in Fresno, California.

For exactly one showing: 2:45 on a Tuesday afternoon.

For a box-office total that came to precisely $48.00.

In today's terms, that would be $56.23.

The reviews were scathing. Actually, no, that's not true: the reviews were nonexistent.

But if the goal for Michaud was, as rumored, for the film to be shown in at least one theater only for it to become eligible for the 1994 Oscars (to take place March 27, 1995), then his goal was successfully accomplished.

But this was just the beginning.

In June 1994, throughout the Los Angeles area, VHS tapes of a strange, very lengthy film began to show up, by mail, to each and every member of the 10,000-strong academy who were eligible to vote.

10,000 VHS tapes.

In a bit of guerrilla marketing years before the term existed, Michaud had the foresight to avoid expensive advertising that went wide, and, instead, go pinpoint and surgical, to reach out to the only people who actually mattered:

The judges, themselves, who voted for the Academy Awards.

As Michaud himself later put it in his self-published memoir, *Winning at Hollywood:* "If they weren't going to see what I created, and it looked like they weren't, then this movie was going to come to them. Just try not watching this film!"

This was not a scam. This was an appeal to Hollywood's heart from a creator with only the best and most earnest of intentions. Michaud genuinely believed he had something very special to offer.

And, in a unique way, he did.

The influence that this (bloated) little movie had on Hollywood and its directors and producers and writers has been written about many times before . . . but I can only stress, once again, how much *This Is How We Love* changed Hollywood forever, just as *Citizen Kane* had in 1941 and *Jaws* did in 1976.

From an oral history on *This Is How We Love,* in the August 2004 issue of *Entertainment Weekly:*

"I hated the movie. Hated it. I don't even remember how I saw it. Maybe on VHS. I think the entire Academy received a VHS copy in the mail. I definitely didn't see it in the theater. But it wouldn't leave my thoughts. I couldn't stop thinking [about] it. That movie opened my mind to the next phase of my career. Batches of characters. Plots interweaving, barely if at all connecting. Characters [who were] 'special.' That's how *Love Actually* came about."
—RICHARD CURTIS

"I don't think it was intentional, but it was the black comedy that appealed to me the most, which is what allowed me to write and direct *American Beauty.*"
—SAM MENDES

"If people think *This Is How We Love* influenced *The Man Without a Face,* they'd be right. I think these are two different, distinct styles of movies, but the overlapping commonality of the facial deformity played not for laughs but for pathos made an important impression on me at that stage of my career."
—MEL GIBSON

"Matt Michaud was an insane person. Nuts. Brilliant. Perhaps he made that film for a tax write-off. Maybe it was a scam. Does it matter? He inadvertently helped foster movies that went on to win awards that would never have won before. In a way, it was as influential as *Jaws.* Think about *Crash. Splanglish. Chocolat. Valentine's Day. Mr. Holland's Opus.* Look at any best-picture winner of the last twenty years: *The English Patient, American Beauty, A Beautiful Mind! The Artist, Birdman.* Some might say we're worse off for it, but, you know, he did what he did. And here we are."

—VIC ROTH, Vanity Fair

"I mean, Jesus Christ! It won the fucking best-picture Academy Award! How fucking cool is that?! People say it didn't win. People also say Marisa Tomei didn't win hers [the award for best supporting actress in 1993 for *My Cousin Vinny*]. Who gives a fuck? In my mind, *This Is How We Love* won. *Forrest Gump* didn't come close! Fuck it!"

—KEVIN SMITH

So there it is. The subject I've been avoiding for the past dozen or so pages (not Kevin Smith's saying "fuck it" for a 2004 *Entertainment Weekly* article) . . . .

Could *This Is How We Love* really and truly have won the best-picture award at the 1994 Academy Awards?!

Could the conspiracy theories actually be . . . true?

Did *This Is How We Love* manage—in an alternative-universe sort of way—to beat out *Forrest Gump,* a film that "officially" took home the best-picture prize, not to mention the hundreds of millions of dollars in box-office receipts?

Was the title *This Is How We Love* read aloud by Al Pacino at the Oscar ceremony, only to then be "corrected" by Robert De Niro, who snatched the card away and loudly announced *Forrest Gump* as that year's best picture?

So many thousands of words have been devoted to this subject that I'm hesitant to dig any deeper into this warmed-over, controversial matter. Snopes.com has come out with an "Unproven" ruling, while one writer for the 1994 Academy Awards, Robert Highson, swears that it's true: "I saw it. It *happened.*"

So where do I come down? More importantly, how do you come down? I mean, do you finally want to discover the answer for yourselves, once and for all?

Yes?

Great!

Well, you can't.

The entire 1994 Academy Awards ceremony is available online. Watch closely and you can detect a noticeable glitch at the three hour, five minute mark, at the very moment the best-picture award winner is announced. Could a tiny portion have been excised from the original, live broadcast? Could a remark or even just a sentence or a movie title have been deleted?

If one were to find the "master tape," held within the library at the Academy's headquarters, in the Samuel Goldwyn Theater, Beverly Hills, one could possibly answer this question officially. But the Academy—so far—has not seen fit to provide permission to access it, even for me and my endless requests.

Especially for me and my endless requests.

Maybe one day.

Until that day, we'll just have to keep piecing together the fragments available in order to form something of a whole. There's been some confusion over how *This Is How We Love* (potentially? allegedly? reportedly?) ever won the best-picture award without ever having been nominated in any category in the first place.

For this delicious brain Twizzler, let's go straight to James Wilkinson, author of 2007's *Hollywood's Greatest Secrets Laid Bare:*

> "This is a movie that was really different. And it had some elements that might have turned people
> off to it—maybe a lot of people. From what I heard, it was a write-in winner for best picture and
> it actually made the list! Like how Donald Duck sometimes wins high-school elections. And then it
> actually won! But a member of the Academy shut that down. How Al Pacino got the card with the
> real winner, and not the winner the Academy wanted, I don't know. But it never made air time. The
> fix is in, as it always is in this country. It had to be *Forrest Gump.* There was never any other choice."

So there it is, folks.

Here's a movie that might or might not have won the best-picture award for 1994.

A movie seen by only around 11,000 people around the world, at the very most, with perhaps five of those people seeing it in the theater upon its initial release.

A movie that doesn't exist these days beyond two or three warbly VHS copies to be found on eBay.

A movie one can only really experience through the 221 film stills in this book.

For what it's worth, Michaud never talked to anyone—reporters or writers—about any of the Oscar rumors, in any interview.

But he did write the following in his self-published memoir:

"I don't know whether [the movie] won the best-picture award or not. Late at night, in my wildest visions, I'll accept the award and thank my parents and friends and the few people who actually saw *This Is How We Love.* Mostly, I thank the filmmakers who were influenced by *Love.* That's the most important aspect. That I made a difference. I'll let the movie do the work for me. All I want these days is to fish and sail on Lake Erie. I'm 60. Let the end credits roll into a new beginning."

In many ways, and certainly in a strange way, Michaud achieved what he had set out to do: make a singular movie that changed cinema on its own terms. Perhaps this meant more to him than any amount of money, which is a rare commodity indeed for a man who started off his career as a scam artist. (His movie benefactor, James Calder Walton, was never reached for comment prior to his death, in 2008, at the age of 86. To this day, it remains unclear whether Walton died satisfied to have made his mark on Hollywood or mortified at how he'd squandered so much of his fortune on the most incoherent disaster in the history of the silver screen. As for what happened to The Rabbit . . . well, let's leave that one alone, shall we?)

What you are holding in your hand is a re-release of the tie-in book that was published in April 1995, shortly after the film won (or didn't win) the best-picture Academy Award. Matthew Michaud himself wrote this book, which he self-published and sent to (you guessed it) all 10,000 members of the voting Academy. This being Hollywood, it's not known how many actually read it, if anyone read it at all.

(While copies of the original first printing of this book are indeed extraordinarily rare, what is not rare are copied versions of the script to the movie itself, which has been performed by various actors and comedians—Paul Rudd, Sarah Silverman, Seth Rogen—at many readings and various events over the years. If there's a reading close to you, by all means go see it!)

Fair warning: All of the "film stills" in this book were actually shot off a VHS bootleg copy of the movie that Michaud owned, hence their opacity. (Why even Michaud himself didn't own a 35-mm print is beyond me!) Also, a few of the shots are in black and white, as the film (at short periods throughout) converts into black and white for "artistic" reasons, similar to Lindsay Anderson's 1968 masterpiece *If . . . .*

Moreover, all of the book's original errors, both grammatical and factual, have been left as is, as has anything that might be construed in modern terms to be "offensive." And yet we've taken great care to vastly improve the quality of the printing and overall design for this new version.

Here is what was in the original version of the book:

221 Movie Stills and Their Captions

Some of the Characters from This Is How We Love *and Their Fascinating Backstories!*

Famous Movie Quotes from the Film

Cast Trivia!

Facts About This Is How We Love

And here is what's new that's included in this 30th-anniversary edition:

This Essay

This Is How We Rub: The 1996 Porn Parody of This Is How We Love

"To Be Honest? We Fucking Hated Each Other!"

An Oral History of Terri Sparks's Final, Disastrous Photo Shoot

Photos from the Terri Sparks Shoot, July 8, 1991

This Is How We Love: *The Official Posters*

So there it is. The story behind *This Is How We Love,* a longtime favorite of mine, even if only in concept, as I've never actually seen it.

In light of this, it thrills me to no end to tell you that I can now actually provide a (potentially) happy ending to this very strange story.

While in the process of doing research for this essay, I learned nothing of the whereabouts of the great Matthew Michaud, or even if he's still alive. He remains a phantom.

But I did come to learn a few things that have never before been reported.

And here is one of them:

When James Calder Walton provided the funds for the making of *This Is How We Love,* in June 1991, he also threw in, for good measure, a number of first-generation Pound Puppies, then still known as "Pound Poochy Pooches." Michaud confirmed as much in his self-published memoir: "When Jim handed me those boxes, I thought he was joking. He said [to me]: 'One day these will be worth a fortune. These are handmade.' I smiled and said nothing. I didn't want to ruin the opportunity to make my movie. But a children's stuffed toy [sic]? Five hundred of them?! Stupid!"

Well . . . maybe not so stupid.

Recently, and out of curiosity, I went onto eBay and typed in "Pound Puppies," and then "Rare."

There was only one seller who apparently specializes in selling first-generation Pound Puppies. Out of the nearly 500 "Original, First-Generation" Pound Puppies this seller owns, 167 have been sold.

For $25,000 each.

Let me repeat that:

For $25,000 each.

For a total of $4,175,000.

The name of the seller?

ThisIsHowWeLove-PoundPuppies-M-Michaud.

I like to imagine that somewhere now on Lake Erie, perhaps on a sailing skiff, perhaps on a fishing boat, Matthew Michaud is, without a doubt, living his best life, rich off the proceeds not from a movie that changed the world but from boxes of first-generation, handmade, floppy-eared, stuffed dogs.

And we should all be right there—on that loamy, foggy shore—waving, smiling . . . rooting this great, odd man on.

Gretchen Millnar

—MARCH 14, 2023

Gretchen Millnar is the author of six books, including the New York Times *bestsellers* Looking Where Others Ain't *and* Raiding a Past to Explore the Future, *both published by Viking Random House. She's a contributor to* Vulture, New York Times, VF.com, Esquire, *and The Onion's AV Club. You can reach her at gretchenmillnar@gmail.com.*

This Is How We Love

AS TOLD THROUGH 221 FILM STILLS AND CAPTIONS

I have helpfully provided you with time stamps to produce a simulation of the excitement and wonder that a first-time viewer must have felt while witnessing the actual movie. I hope you will delight in what I have directed and written! Grab a bucket of popcorn and enjoy!

—MATTHEW MICHAUD, writer/director for *This Is How We Love*

00:01:35   Just a typical street in a typical American town: Brentwood, Los
            Angeles. On a clear day, the gorgeous Santa Monica Mountains
            are visible. This is where the entirety of the film takes place. It's
            practically "Everywhere, USA!"

00:02:04   The homeless man, Klat, who shows up out of the blue to live in front of the compound owned by the Adams family. What is he doing in Brentwood? And why does he have a Playboy-insignia tattooed on his forehead? Is he dangerous? Or just eccentrically wise?

00:03:29   "I no have good feeling about man without home, señor," says Ray Ray the Hispanic gardener to his boss, Bizz Adams, former astronaut. "No, no. No! No! No! No! No, señor!"

00:05:01   "Honey, I may have been to the moon as an astronaut . . . but I still can't flip a pancake!" proclaims Bizz.

00:05:13　"Don't say Hispanics are lazy, Momma! That's just not true! And you know it! Ray Ray has worked *very* hard for us! He's the best gardener we could have possibly found not going through a legal agency."

00:05:17 The swirling stack of trash that represents the transitory nature of life. Throughout the film, this shot will appear any time a character comes to an epiphany.

00:05:38　Azure Adams, gorgeous, alcoholic wife of once famous astronaut Bizz Adams: "You've been to the moon, Bizz, but you are unable to achieve *emotional* liftoff! Admit it, Bizz, you chose the *moon* over *me*! Can I not compare to the moon?! Are you unable to land on me?"

00:05:43   "Just one more nip before lunch. That's all. It won't hurt a soul. Least of all *mine*! As my sponsor likes to say, '*Condom's up!*'"

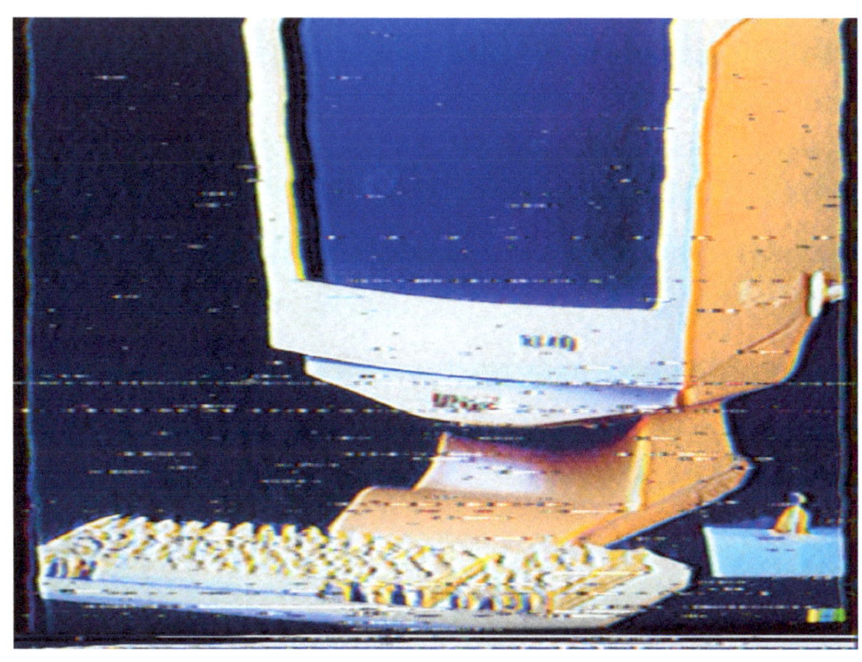

00:06:17   The computer that the Hawaiian-shirt-wearing teen uses to hack
into the CIA's mainframe "system."

00:07:08   Melissa Adams, troubled grown daughter of Azure and Bizz.
             Could it be time for an intensive makeover? She is a stutterer and,
             unfortunately, a "lesbian."

00:07:15   Bobby Adams, brother of Melissa Adams' and the son of Bizz and
Azure. He is a former race car driver with half his face burned off.
Now he has an exciting new dream that, in some ways, will be just
as thrilling as professional NASCAR racing: "I will be a Brentwood
real estate agent. This world will *never* stop me. It *will* happen!"

00:09:40　　Suffering from depression, Melissa volunteers at a suicide hotline. Most of the callers end up talking her out of taking her own life . . . although five do urge her to go through with it.

Vicky, Melissa Adams' live-and-let-live roommate. She is in the
swing dancing group "Swing Squad." Her boyfriend, Topper, is
a skateboard messenger who mistakenly stumbles upon a legal
document that could very well threaten the world's rainforests. In his
free time, Topper loves "blading" to Blockbuster's.

00:11:31   Ray Ray, the Mexican gardener belonging to Bizz and Azure Adams. He works very, very hard under a blazing hot sun without bothersome complaint.

00:12:55   "The thing I hate about people who kill themselves is the bloody mess they leave behind!" screams Azure Adams to her daughter, Melissa, about those unfortunates who are "depressed."

00:13:26   Ray Ray the Gardener's wife and the household cook, Angel, often called by the Adams family: "*Our* Angel." She doesn't yet know that her husband is having a torrid affair with her racist boss, Azure.

00:15:22   Flatthery, the youngest son of Bobby Adams. Fully deaf, he longs to one day hear a grunge song written about him. He spends hour upon hour gazing at the Stone Temple Pilots poster above his bed, daydreaming about the full spectrum of Scott Weiland's vocal capabilities.

00:17:45   "I know, daddy, I know! I *know* we have to talk about mother! I
             know she's drinking too much! I know! I *know*! I *KNOW*!!!"

00:19:12   Manuel, the schizophrenic son of Ray Ray the gardener and Angel
the house cook. Haunted by voices, Manuel decides to attend
community college to study advanced physics. But will his genius
and ferocious drive guide him through? The doctors doubt it.

00:21:19   Alone with his memories, former astronaut Bizz watches old
            Super-8 home movies of his life before it all became so complicated
            and suburbanly sad.

00:23:15   "I love you, too. But you're just too . . . promiscuous for someone so mediocre looking."

00:26:53   The 1975 Bentley Corniche, capable of only making right turns.

00:28:19   George the black "gang banger" who is involved in the auto accident with Bizz. Uh oh! Will they come to blows?!

"I'll pay for your child's education at the local community college," generously declares Azure to her Hispanic cook, Angel. "It's the least I can do. I guess."

00:33:50   "Why do you call me 'dawg'? As a form of endearment?" inquires
Bizz to his new black pal George the Gang Banger.

00:37:04   Azure's drinking scares all the household's pets . . . and quite a few of
             the wild animals in the extensive, manicured backyard.

00:39:56   Bobby Adams, oldest son of Bizz and Azure. Unfortunately, half his face is burned off very badly because of a race car incident years before.

00:40:05   Bobby flashes back to his NASCAR racing accident involving the
            baby who crawled onto the track. The baby survives! But Bobby
            is trapped inside his car and forever and terribly scarred. Bobby
            tragically loses his Mello Yello sponsorship.

00:41:25 "That's odd. I always thought your face was grotesquely burned because of a cigar bar accident."

00:41:27   "No."

   Ray Ray the Hispanic gardener attempts to teach Azure how to make *corn tortillas*. Perhaps they have more in common than frantic sex on a bed of cut grass in the shed?

00:44:56   Later that afternoon: Ray Ray raises the squirrel back from the dead
with a little help from his knowledge of the mysterious religion of
the primitives, Santeria.

00:45:50   "Ever since you were shot in the head during that robbery gone wrong, you've been . . . just a whole lot nicer!" says Vicky to her Gen-Z boyfriend Topper.

00:47:02   "Momma, I made three new friends at college today!" brags
schizophrenic Manuel to his mother Angel. But *did* he?

00:49:18   Complaining all the way, Bizz is forced to learn "sign language" to communicate with his deaf grandson, Flatthery. It's the *last* thing he wants to do! What a waste of time!

00:49:59   Melissa Adams comes clean with her secret. Not only is she, herself, suicidal, but she is also a stutterer. Moreover, she is a fan of "goth" music. And she enjoys the sexual company of women.

00:51:47 "He's saying that 'He didn't steal nothin.' But *someone* is stealing from my luxury soap store! And it *has* to be Wesley, the only black on staff!" extorts Maraket Adams, Bizz's sister.

00:53:04   Timmy, the eldest son of Bobby the former race car driver, arrives home after a year of touring the world as a famous grunge rock "n" roll singer. He wears jeans with rips. There is no seamstress for *this* band!

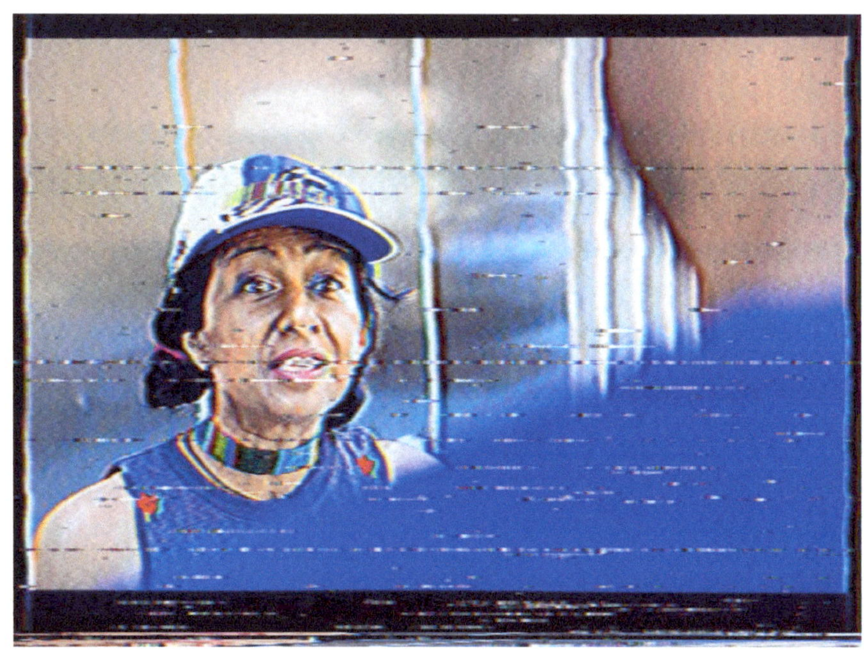

00:58:07   Melissa's best friend and roommate Vicky. She longs to one day win big at a Swing Dancing Championship. But she has a club foot. And is dating Topper, who is too apathetic to dance.

01:01:05   "Your name. It *fizzes* on my tongue." Topper has a way with words. He's a Gen-X poet.

01:03:05 "Marcus is all juss mix up,' exclaims his mother to the white store worker at the luxury soap store. 'He ain't no criminal! He . . . he just an *artist*! Are you sure it wasn't the black worker?'"

01:03:07   "My son is a genius! See what I mean?"

01:03:18   "My mom, she has a tendency to *over* exaggerate. Except in this case.
I am a genius, yeah."

01:05:36   "I'll slug you as sure as God made sour apples!" pronounces Bobby the former NASCAR driver. This is how *real* men talk.

01:07:09   "Anyone seen my sobriety coin? I wanna buy more booze."

01:09:23   Manuel hits the wild community college dance club circuit with his three best new buds: Tony, Harold and Victor. "Friendship is paradise!" But *is* it?

01:13:40   Bizz, Bobby, Azure and Rachey supper together as a family. Only the scraping of plates can be heard, very little conversation: "How was your day?" "*Fine.*"

01:15:02   Black "gang banger" George and former astronaut Bizz talk poolside
about the local major league baseball team, the Los Angeles Dodgers.
Perhaps they're not so *different* after all?

01:20:07   "Why do you call me, 'spaceman'? Is that an urban form of
                  endearment?"

01:21:09   "Please quit your McJob at the McGap! No more McDreams! Follow your most *sincere* passion of opening that high-end hip-hop apparel themed store on Rodeo Drive! It *can't* fail!"

01:26:47   Rachey Abrams, gorgeous middle-aged wife of Bobby the former NASCAR driver. Although already in her late-twenties, she is extremely beautiful. She is also an escort specializing in suburbal sexual acts.

01:29:22   Homeless man Klat still lives outside the compound at the foot of
the driveway. Although without a house, he is extremely wise. His
unbridled screaming can change the lives of those willing to listen.

01:30:07   "What are you *hiding*?!"

01:30:26   "Sometimes a man has to lose *everything* before he gains a drop of *wisdom*. And let me tell you, I am *ejaculating* wisdom right now!"

01:32:41   Bones, the blind dog. He can "see" more clearly than most humans.

01:33:08   "So the dog is blind but he can somehow *see*? How the hell does that work?"

01:35:53   The empty porch swing.

01:36:12   The unsent letter.

01:38:22   "What I find interesting, Bizz, is that you've been to the moon but still are impotent. Why are you unable to plant your flag in *me*?"

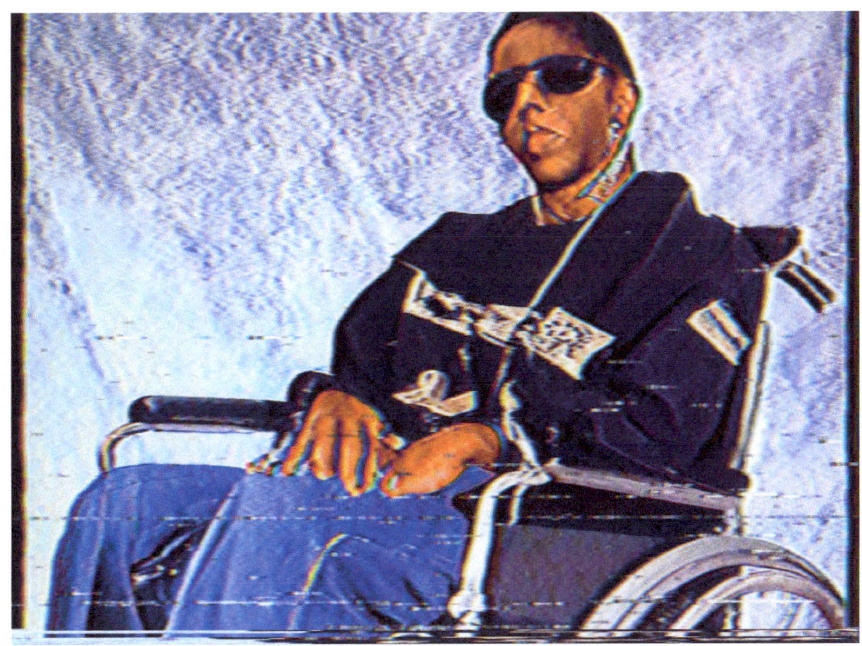

01:44:33   Donald, the pimp with cerebral palsy, who does not let his disability interfere with his stern hand or deep love of feministic values.

01:50:11   Manuel's second "friend" Tony attempts to assassinate the college
            dean by dropping poison into his expensive espresso martini.

01:53:55   Rachey Abrams, gorgeous middle-aged wife of Bobby the former NASCAR driver, out for drinks alone, flirts with a handsome man who is unaware she is married. It is Robbie Hostetleir of the Denver Broncos. But Hostetleir takes it too far. The flirts cross the *line*."

01:54:21   Luckily, black gang banger George, out for a night of "wilding," is at
            the right place to stop the unwanted shenanigans!

01:56:10   "*What do I want?* I want to become the most successful real-estate agent Brentwood has *ever* seen! But I have a slight problem . . . *half my face is burned off!*"

01:57:29 Bizz is a fiend for the jigsaw puzzle. But there's *one* particular jigsaw puzzle he just can't seem to tackle. It frustrates him *very* much.

01:58:56   The ethnic neighbors, the Schwartzmanns, who are capable of
            showing so much more emotion than the Adams.

01:59:33   "Bones the dog! He's gone! *Vanished*!" squeals Flatthery the deaf boy too loudly.

02:02:03   "Don't you *dare* blame Klat for Bones's disappearance! He may be
homeless but he wouldn't hurt a kitten!"

02:02:21   "Oh my Lord! Klat just *killed* a kitten!"

02:03:13   "Daddy, I was so, *so* tired of the Grunge life! That's why I've come back *home*!"

02:03:14 "What's the *real* reason?"

02:03:16   "I'm on illegal drugs, okay! And . . . I just can't seem to *stop,* daddy!"

02:04:10   The itinerant band of hippies cavorting in the kidney-shaped pool.

02:07:21 "Please don't kill yourself. I'm begging you. We all have our burdens to bear. Can I tell you mine? I'm suicidal. And I s–s–s–s–s–s–stutter!"

02:07:23　　　"I can't believe she k-k-k-k-k-k-killed herself."

02:08:43　　"The last thing I want is to adopt another goddamn *child*! Who need's em?! Especially when they're fully fuckin' *grown*!"

02:09:31   The documents proving that Klat was once an extremely successful millionaire businessman. *But why?* And how did he end up *shoeless*, living in front of the Adams' family compound? It's all such a baffling, delicous mystery!

02:11:00   The priceless Steuben glass egg that sits on the mantelpiece in the Adams' living room. Azure makes it clear that if anything happens to it, she will *not* be happy!

02:12:02   "You are not like the other Mexicans, Ray Ray. I don't know, you're just . . . *different.* Less ethnic. More willing ... to sleep with me."

02:13:10 "My *abuela* was so strong, so proud. Her wisdom is as close to me as this here *margarita*," tenderly explains Mexican gardener Ray Ray. To prove his confused point, Ray Ray downs his margarita in one long, forceful gulp.

02:15:48   "Wanna go halfsies on a baby?" Rachey inquires of Bobby, her
burnt-faced husband. "Let's do this!!!!!!!!"

02:17:04   "I'm sorry, ma'am. There are no more babies. How would you like
a grown Indian with intellectual disabilities? His family died last year
in a forest fire because of greedy developers," explains the assistant
manager of the adoption center.

02:17:11   A doe denning 'neath the moonlight.

02:17:30   "You've got to be kidding me! I don't want another kid! Especially
an Indian adult, for crying out loud!!!"

02:17:36   "He's no different than *anyone* else! But even if so, it's the differences that bring us *together*! Especially environmental issues that could effect white people like ourselves!"

02:17:39   "His name is Pecker, woman!"

02:17:52   "Yes! Short for 'Peckerwood! *Nature!*"

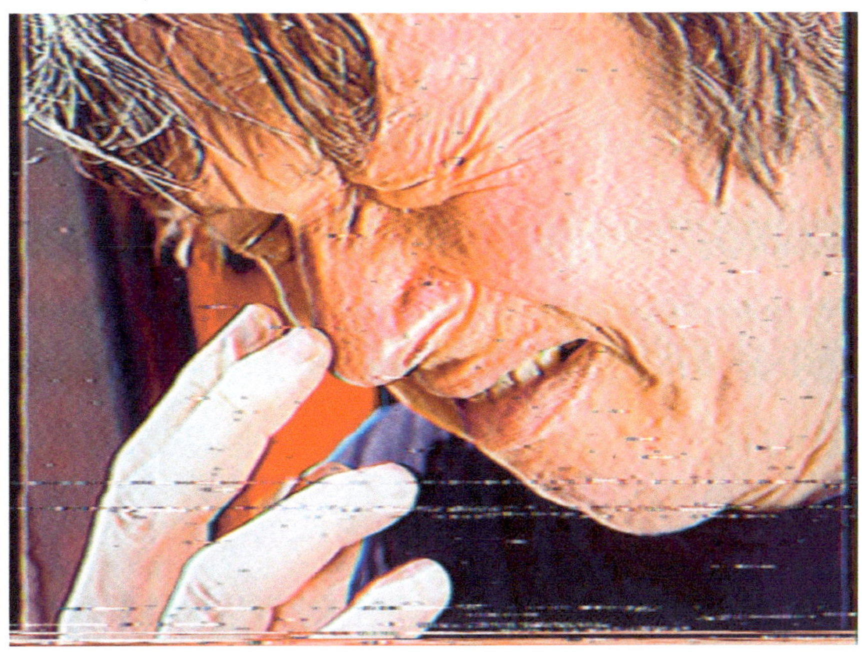

02:18:02   "Honey, my tests came back. The one for AIDS."

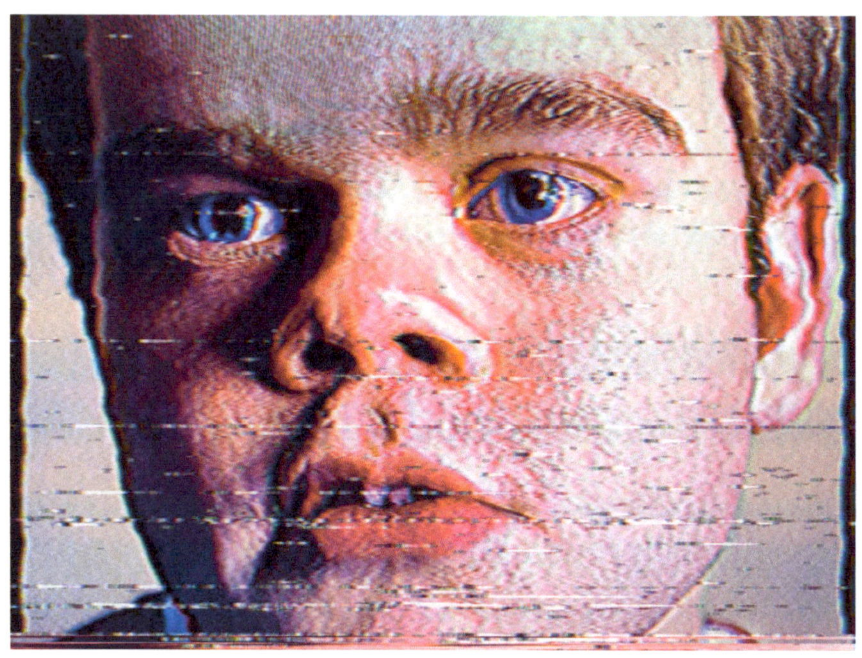

02:18:43   "Mommy, do angels yawn?"

02:19:54   "Blood on my knife or shit on my dick, I *will* collect what I'm owed."

02:20:58   Former astronaut Bizz pumps iron. Is he having an affair? What could be the *real* reason behind these nighttime garage workouts?

"I would love to teach you how to play soccer, señor Bizz, *si si si*!" exlaims Ray Ray in heavily accented English. "*Si si*, most indeed!"

02:23:05   "That's where I get my inspiration," says George, pointing to the
heavens. "The Big Dawg."

 The priceless signed and framed self-portrait by John Lennon as seen hanging in the foyer of the Adams' residence. It means everything to Bizz, even though he does disagree with the sentiments in "Imagine" and "Give Peace a Chance."

02:25:13   "I was a better man with you as a woman than I ever was with a
woman as a man who wanted to be a woman but felt more like a
man than he ever felt as a woman."

02:27:20   Harold, one of Manuel's three community college "buds," plants a
bomb beneath the dean's bicycle. Or has he?

02:28:04   "I just want to take off this outfit and perform my vulgar, whorish business while fantasizing about state-of-the-art skin grafts that will soon restore my husband's freakishly burned face."

02:28:31 Reading an old diary, Azure learns that her mother, Mildred, perished after escaping Auschwitz while pregnant and then giving birth inside a Nazi barn. *What?!* Azure is one-half Jewish?! It's just too much, being *ambushed* like this!

02:30:47   Victor, Manuel's third college "friend," shoots out the dean's
           expensive Honda Accord's car tires with a .22 rifle.

02:31:14   "That baby you saved on the NASCAR track, do you remember her?"

02:31:17   "No. *Why*?"

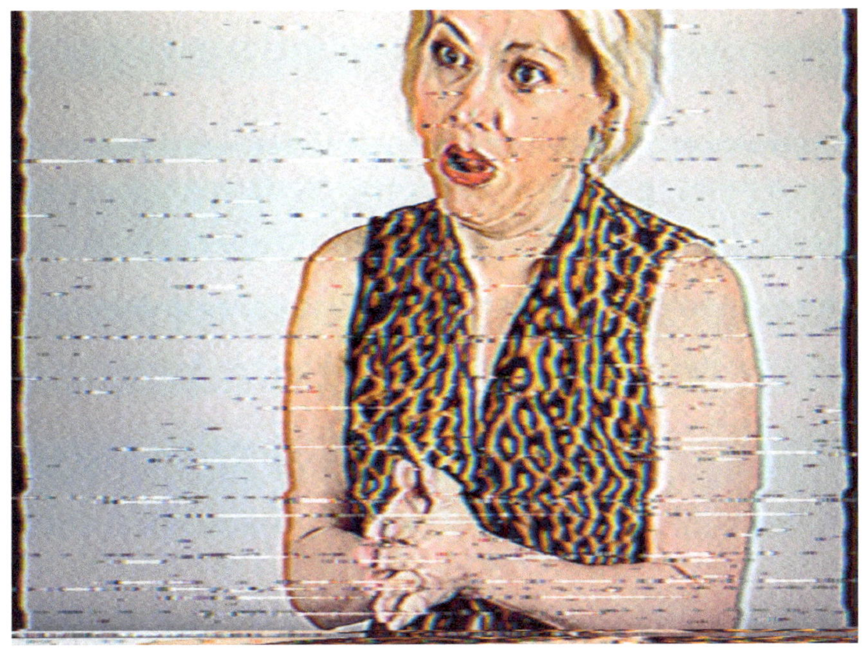

"She's now Dr. Vaughan, a cosmetic surgeon! World famous! And she wants to fix your face!! *Nothing's gonna stop you from selling as many expensive homes in Brentwood as you have your heart set on!*"

02:33:14   The spilled bottle of Valium.

02:33:23   "Charles Bukowski! He's a poet, a warrior, a scoundrel, he's my
            Gen-X *god*!"

02:33:43   Matthew, gay son of the ethnic neighbors, the Schwartzmanns.
            He loves to cook and design Internet "Web Sites" waherein blue
            "hyperlinks" turn purple when one activates them or "clicks."

02:34:10   The extraordinarily high–tech Casio QV-10 digital video recorder.

02:34:30   Out for a "walkabout" in the woods, perhaps hunting for squirrel, the adopted Indian Pecker stumbles across the blind dog Bones, trapped beneath a sewer line next to the electrical towers.

02:34:33   Thunder and lightning.

02:35:02   In the nick of time, Bones the blind dog is saved by the adopted
            Indian Peckerwood.

02:36:52   "I told you he was *special! Now* are you happy we adopted a fully grown Indian with severe emotional issues?"

02:37:32   The wise homeless man Klat is invited *inside* the compound for the annual Adams' Family Christmas party! He even wears socks!

138

02:41:11   The mother of the white thief and artist, Marcus, the morning after
            her terrible catatonic encephalitis diagnosis—she's about to disappear
            into her own mind! Despite full body spasms, she'll soon manage to
            slow-dance with her bald neurologist.

02:43:08   Bones takes an immediate shine to homeless man Klat. Perhaps this dog can "see" the wisdom in Klat that humans tend to miss?

02:43:15   But Bones is still a bit leery. Might he sniff out a secret?

02:43:21 "Could the cause of your stuttering be due to your issues of lesbianism?" inquires well-meaning Angel. Although a wonderful cook for the Adams family, Angel can sometimes be too ethnically "direct" in her questioning.

02:43:34   "That's it! Get *angry*! Get *furious*! I'm *fucking* the gardener! And he's *brown*!" clucks Bizz's wife Azure. Is this *her* talking? Or the six *appletinis* she's had since supper?

02:43:52 "Manuel, your friends *don't* exist. It was *you* who shot the gun! It was *you* who lit the bomb! It was *you* who stole the kitchen knife! It was *you* all along! You're *sick*! Honey, you need *help* from a balding psychiatrist in a sweater!"

02:44:01   "My biggest dream? To open a hacky sack store and an umbrella-hat kiosk in the mall. Come *mall* with me!"

02:44:09 Biz realizes he *does* adore his wife, despite her terrible alcoholism and anger issues and sexual impropriety and anything else that medical professionals might refer to as "tolerable behavior." "I know I shouldn't love her but I've never let knowledge stop me before!"

02:44:37   Melissa befriends gay neighbor, Matthew Schwartzmann. They have much to *chitty-chat* and *tittle-tattle* about!

 Bizz speaks with his neighbor Arnold Schwartzmann about Arnold's gay son. "I've been to the moon, Arnold, and I can tell you that space does not care one iota about sexuality. If the moon were a homosexual, the sun wouldn't mind. That's just how space works."

02:45:13   In a flashback to June 1942, we see how Azure's mother Mildred
             falls in love with Fritz, a kind Nazi guard who for months hands her
             a single red rose each morning through the barbed wire before roll
             call. She's already pregnant with Azure.

02:45:21   Fritz the Nazi entertains lucky concentration campers with his unique, hilarious antics!

02:45:36   Nazi Fritz is murdered by Nazi leadership for not being strict enough. With his demise, it's now impossible for Jews to ignore the subpar conditions of Auschwitz.

02:45:48　　After her escape during Fritz's torture, and before giving birth to Azure, Mildred becomes a world-famous World War II nurse, the subject of many a song and Hebrew poem.

02:46:02   Does Bizz *himself* have something to hide?!

02:46:03   He does! "My friends who died in space! It was because of *me*! I lit
           that cigar to celebrate when we landed! Perhaps that was a *mistake*!"

02:46:04   "It's not because you are gay?"

02:46:05   "Huh?"

02:46:17   Bizz's daughter Melissa Adams churbles: "And that's why you've never been able to achieve full emotional liftoff, daddy! Because you killed people on the moon!"

02:46:21 "That and crash-landing in a school playground, killing 25 children," Azure adds helpfully.

02:46:29   "We can't sleep together, Ray Ray! I learned that I love Bizz more than I ever thought. And he's getting back into astronaut shape for me. *Me!* Goodbye! You can still work as my gardener with no medical benefits!"

02:46:31   Bizz at last achieves *full* "emotional liftoff." It's all so *clear* now! To prove as much, the trash swirls!

02:47:02   "I understand that my son is gay but that does not mean he is no
            longer my son. I have so much to learn. Thank you, Bizz, for your
            out-of-this-earth wisdom."

<table>
<tr><td>02:49:12</td><td>Bobby meets with the person he saved on the NASCAR track who is now a very pricey cosmetic surgeon who has been featured in a three-page paid advertisement in Vanity Fair and who is married to an Asian.</td></tr>
</table>

02:50:04   "It's so costly, babe. I just don't know if we can *afford* this . . . I know it's your face, but is there a—um, perhaps—cheaper route we could take with all this?"

02:52:29   "Maybe I can help . . . " exclaims Rachey later that night, shocking
them all.

02:52:31   "Actually, it *is* really expensive. Sorry. I can't."

02:54:05   "*I'll* pay for it," says Klat even later that night.

02:54:07　　　“Who *are* you?”

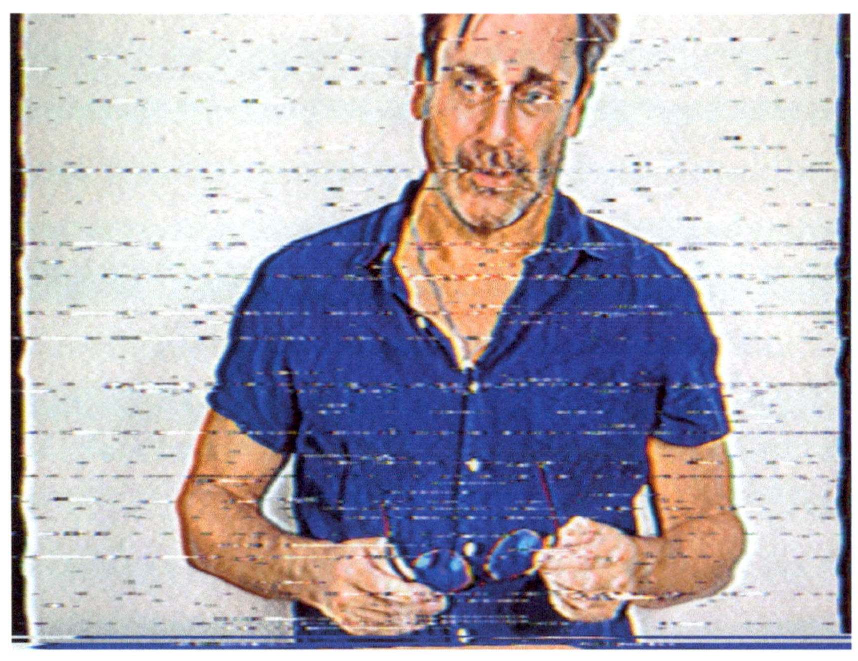

02:56:17   "I think my heart is back open for business!"

02:59:17   The next morning, Timmy promises to never again play grunge music—at least until he kicks the illegal drugs that make him too logy even for the grunge.

02:59:37   "You're not mad at me? For sleeping with *your* husband and *my* gardener?" Azure gently inquires of Angel, her illegal alien cook.

03:02:56   Angel is not mad for long! Hispanics are unable to *stay* mad! To show her appreciation, Azure teaches Angel a little something special about *her* culture: how to make fried Zucchini Zircles with a mayonnaise- and cinnamon-based dip.

03:03:03   In a dream sequence: Mirakle . . . a woman who would have been twenty-six if Azure hadn't aborted her all those years ago.

03:06:13   "Pecker is *my* son! I was too ashamed to tell anyone! I met his mother on the reservation after I crash–landed for the third time in June 1972!"

173

03:07:45   Bizz breaks into a coughing fit.

03:08:15   When not "blading" or skateboarding, Topper enjoys growing illegal
             marijuana.

03:09:32   Having memorized every observable comet in history, Peckerwood tells the family about the Big One (or the "Comet of Icy Fire") to arrive later that week.

03:10:18   Peckerwood volunteers as a volunteer fireman. He's ready to become a hero!

03:10:25   Bobby's facial surgery is a *major* success thanks to a former millionaire who now finds himself homeless in a Brentwood, Los Angeles compound. But the question remains: *Who is Klat and what is he doing living at the base of the Adams' winding driveway without shoes?*

03:10:33   "Mrs. Adams, you are the most amazing white woman I ever did
have miscegenation carnal relations with!" eagerly proclaims the
Mexican gardener Ray Ray. The sweat on his brow is clearly visible.

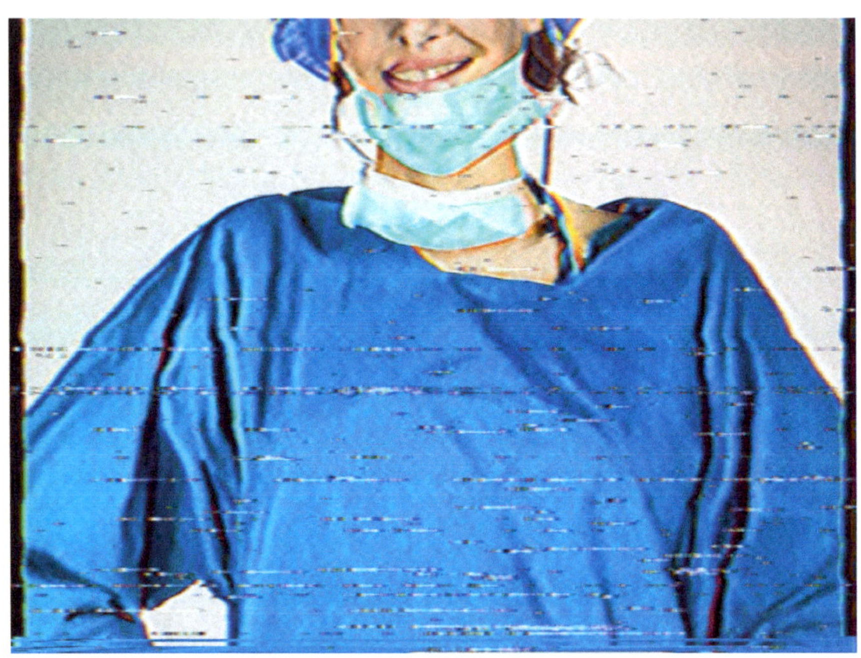

03:11:21   The next day: "I'm so happy you're okay with your new face! Thank you for saving me as a baby! My husband is *also* a world-famous surgeon! But he specializes in *ears*. Would you like your deaf son to once again hear like he did before his midnight-rave-in-a-cornfield accident?"

03:12:18   "We should talk about this. This ear surgeon just happens to be . . . *Asian*."

03:12:43   "But if he doesn't, he'll never be able to hear music! *My* music!"

03:13:12   Flatterhy listens to the special grunge ditty that his older brother
             Timmy just wrote about *him* and recorded that morning. It is
             exquisite! Even when he imagined this song in his head, it wasn't as
             delicious as this! How *could* it have been?!

03:13:45   The framed gold grunge record. It did not take long for Timmy's new grunge song to go "gold."

03:15:56   The outdoor concert on July 4th that features famous rock star
Kenny Loggins performing alongside Timmy . . . *in front of Flatterhy,
who has scored a front row seat!*

03:16:11   Melissa plans to work just *one more night* at the suicide hotline.

03:17:07   In an incredible coincidence, Melissa's mother Azure happens to be Melissa's very *last* suicide call! "Momma? Is that you?! Why do you wish to kill yourself?"

03:17:11   "You saved my life, honey!"

03:17:27   "I'm ashamed of the way I acted. The racism. The hatred. My inner darkness. The infidelity. No more drinking! That starts tomorrow! I'm too drunk now!"

03:18:27 "And because of saving my momma's life, and the elocution course on compact disc, my stutter vanquished! I can now quit this job! And do what I always *wanted*! Something actually *important*! Teaching algebra to inner-city kids who don't want to learn it."

03:19:17   The look on his younger brother's face does the trick! "The only drug I truly need from now on is to make people happy with my grunge!" articulates Timmy with great passion.

03:19:43   Melissa questions Klate outside the family compound. "A helicopter accident in South Africa?! And you were the pilot?! *That's* why you're homeless?!"

03:20:04 Klat recounts for Melissa the entire narrative of the diamond–
        smuggling ring back in South Africa all those years ago.

03:21:04   The next day, Melissa is ecstatic. "The job I *always* wanted! To teach troubled inner-city colored youth 8th grade advanced algebra! I just hope as a *white woman* I can connect with them!"

03:21:35   George the black gang banger finds himself in Melissa's algebra class.
It just so happens that he is a genius when it comes to mathematics.
He drops the knife that he was about to use for nefarious purposes
. . . and tends to those who are younger and more vulnerable
and willing to transform from underperformers into a class of
*over*achievers!

03:23:15   Azure convinces Klat to take her husband up into the sky for a
            ride in a helicopter. Klat can fly the helicopter and Bizz can be the
            passenger! Maybe it'll do them *both* a world of good!

03:26:24   Klat rents a helicopter and takes Bizz for a ride. Even though he's already been to the moon, there's just something about helicopters that scares Bizz to near death . . .

03:27:12   Uh oh! While piloting the helicopter, Klat suffers a heart attack . . .

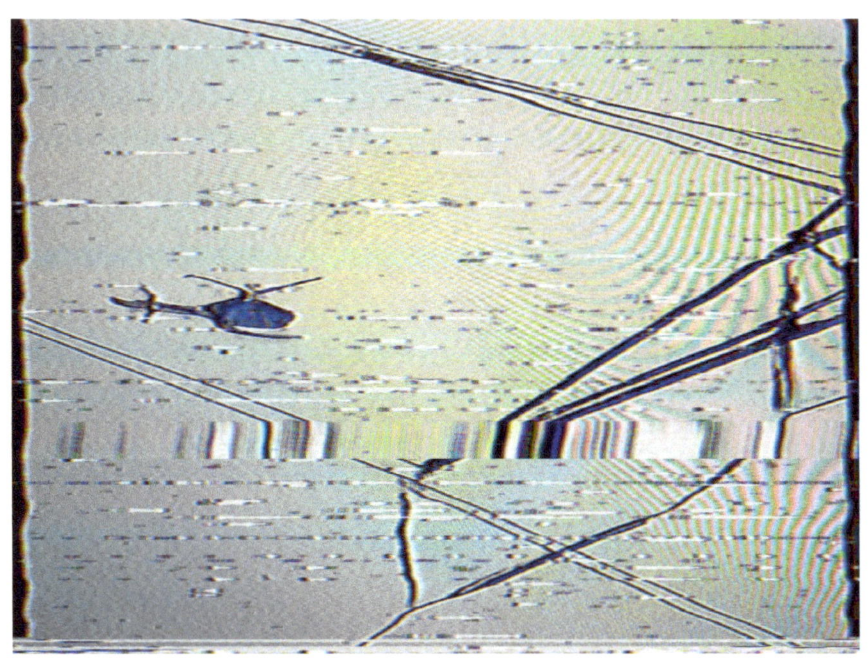

03:27:16   Out of control and headed straight for the power lines . . . this looks bad! . . .

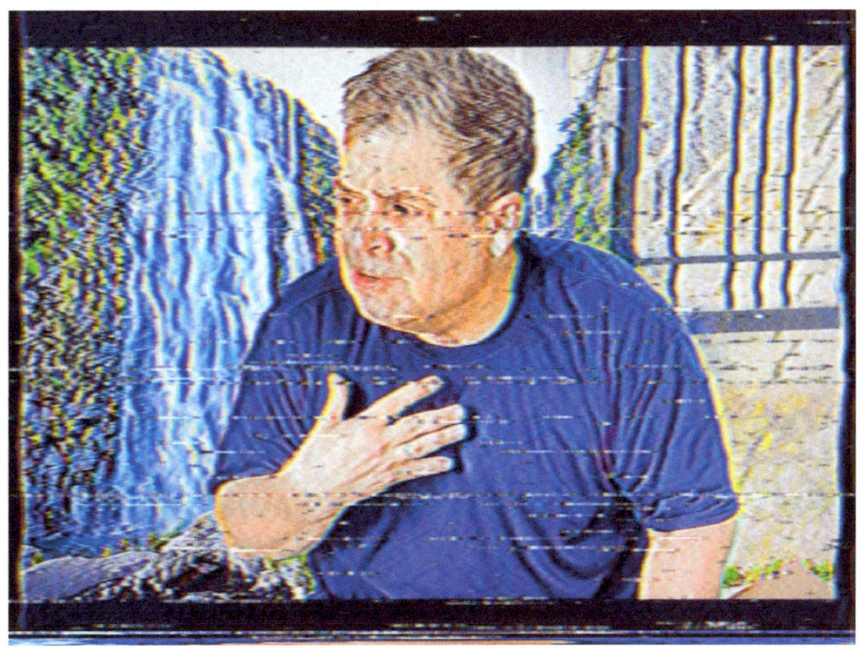

03:27:22   Klat flashes back to another helicopter crash years ago in South
             Africa.

03:27:28   Within the same flashback, a younger Klat steers his helicopter straight into a dangerous waterfall to impress a gorgeous blonde Afrikaner. He is saved by a group of shirtless surfers! He crashes. And becomes homeless. *That's* the reason!

03:27:44   Now it's Bizz's turn to flashback . . .

03:28:18   "We landed on the moon! Time to celebrate with a cigar inside an oxygen-rich spacecraft with best buds!" asserts a younger and more confident Bizz.

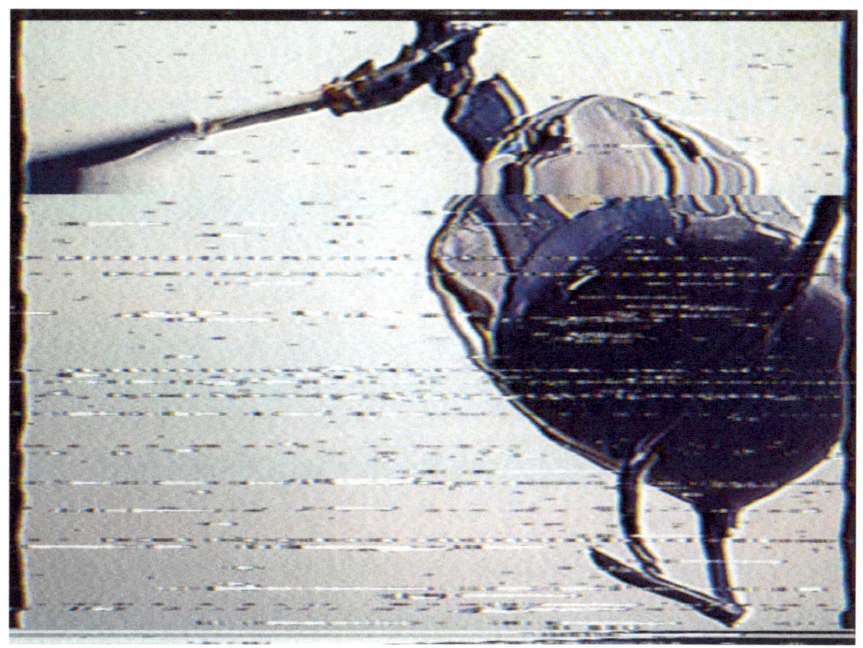

03:29:02   In the present day, the helicopter plunges with Klat and Bizz in it
. . . "Bizz, you gotta fly this bird like the astronaut I *know* you are."

03:29:22   The schizophrenic Manuel (while out shopping for a gold fanny
            pack in downtown Brentwood) notices what is happening with Klat
            and Bizz up in the rented helicopter!

03:29:26   Shouting, not always comprehensibly, Manuel explains to them both how to land safely. His tremendous knowledge of community college physics helps enormously.

03:29:44   The helicopter lands safely on the ethnic Schwartzmann's lawn. *Klat has merely faked his heart attack in order for Bizz to regain his confidence!* And homosexual Matthew is there to greet them with his mouthwatering hors d'oeuvres! It turns out that he simply is a *fabulous* cook!

03:29:58   Manuel sends Tony, Harold and Victor packing and out of his brain. He no longer needs their help, thank you very much! He can do all this on his own! Real friends are so much *cooler* than imagined ones!

03:30:08   "I think we are *both* outliers," says Manuel to Matthew. "Me crazy, you gay. These coconut shrimp buttons are *yummers*! You should start your own catering business! Maybe Angel the Latino cook could help! She could use more work!"

03:31:18   The vice principal casts a glance that lingers just a tad too long for it to be a mistake. Perhaps there *is* something between Melissa and this very attractive middle-aged woman who never married and calls herself "Butch"?

03:32:06   No longer impotent, Bizz has so much to look forward to! Except for this stubborn cough . . .

03:33:34 Bobby surveys (from the helicopter that Klat is piloting) all of the expensive Brentwood homes he intends to now sell. Klat is officially Bobby's employee! "This is pure *magic*! My new, better face, it's . . . it's a *gold mine*!"

03:33:45   Dropping the advertising leaflets! "This is for *you*, Brentwood!"

03:34:23   The ultra–modern black Nokia 440 portable mobile telephone.

03:35:12	Timmy starts his first day at Ragged Jeans, his very own grunge record label.

03:35:45 Formerly deaf younger brother Flatterhy stops by to help and suggest awesome "chord changes"! "Hear how that *sounds*?! Every grunge god has these memorized, dude!"

03:35:53   Flatterhy just cannot stop playing! This grunge sounds *amazing*!!!

03:36:22   Melissa also makes a stop at Ragged Jeans.

03:36:53   "Who's placing the bag of excrement inside the school cafeteria?
Could it be the brain-damaged janitor who lives in the secret room
above the girls' lockers?"

03:36:59   "No. It was just Carl, the head of the civics department. The Gulf War has affected him terribly."

03:37:02   "The trouble with history is that you have to live through it.
Momma needs a freshie. And make 'er *sing*!"

03:37:15   Melissa convinces her nephew Timmy the rocker to come to her classroom. Algebra is so much *easier* to learn with the help of some grunge! The ghetto children love it!

03:37:52   Taking only right turns with the Bentley, Azure pays a visit to her daughter's inner-city classroom . . . and truly *likes* what she sees . . . but can't later remember.

03:38:12   The character of Brick, who doesn't appear in the final cut of the film, in a casket after committing suicide, his bedroom filled with trophies that remain untouched. The character was a promising college student–athlete who sank too deep into a cult and drank poison at a gathering of people it turns out were not his *true* friends.

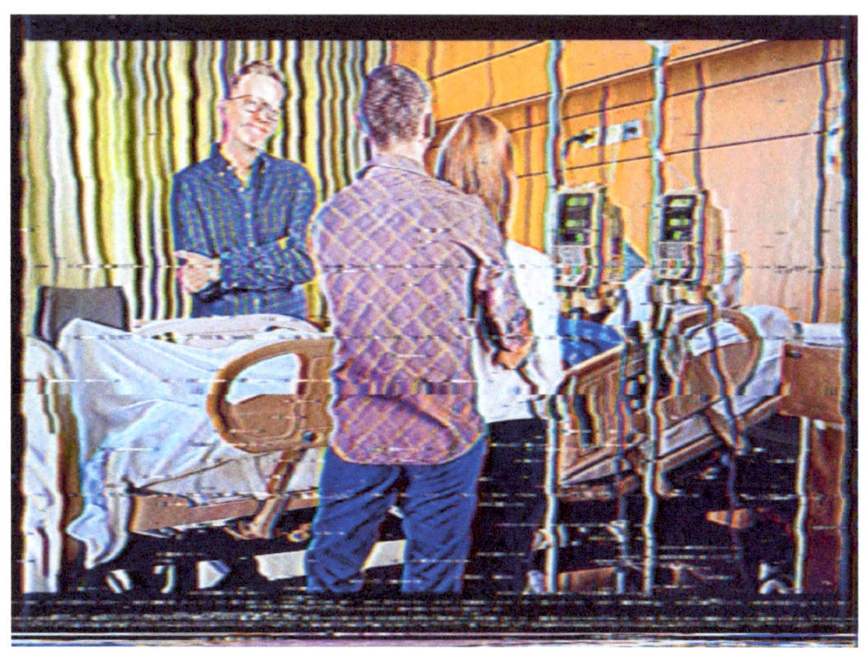

03:38:42 Bizz is surrounded by family in the hospital, dying of lung cancer. He's been to the moon. He's landed an out-of-control helicopter. Next to him is a framed work of art of his entire family . . . as painted by Marcus, the white thief from Maraket's artisanal, luxury soap store.

03:38:47   Also included in the painting . . . former homeless man, Klat, who now lives *inside* the compound, above the garage, away from the rest of the family, in an unfurnished, barely-heated apartment that stores the family's Super-8 home vintage pornography movie collection. *Heaven*!

03:39:53   Later that night: "There was always one jigsaw puzzle daddy could never *quite* figure out."

03:40:12   "It was a puzzle of an Earth photo as shot from space!"

03:40:24   "Let's put the puzzle together. *As a family.*"

03:41:12 "George places the very last piece into the puzzle. The black gang banger has shockingly solved it! *It is the Earth as shot from space!!!*"

03:42:05 The half-eaten celebratory cake from Michelin-star awarded Brentwood bakery Upscale Confections, as now run by gay, ethnic neighbor Matthew. A full-page advertisement about the bakery will soon be featured in *Vanity Fair*!

03:42:45   The unwatered ficus tree once again showing signs of life. It *has* to be a miracle!

03:43:11   With Topper's winnings from the World Ring-Frisbee Toss
Championship Tournament, both he and Vicky set off to live a very
happy life even deeper into the suburbs.

03:44:12   George breaks down crying—but in his own "urban" way. "Yo! I
           guess we all just our own type of 'dawgs.'"

03:44:57   The family slow-dances as one to "Orinoco Flow."

03:45:13   The lesbian vice principal, Kirsty Mallano, expresses a word of
             kindness to the student in the germ-free plastic bubble.

03:46:13 The lesbian vice principal, Kirsty Mallano, in death, after catching a disease from the allegedly germ-free boy. Perhaps she can *now* find peace?

03:46:50   "Life is a rollercoaster, honey. But wouldn't you rather ride a water-
slide with me acting as the water? That's a metaphor. Honey?"

03:47:02   The family stares at the Comet of Icy Fire that Peckerwood
accurately predicted would arrive at exactly 11:04 PM.

03:47:12   The grandfather clock symbolically stuck at 11:04 PM.

03:47:52   The film's narrator all along has been Peckerwood, now a heroic fireman in Brentwood. His audience is other firemen. They listen in *awe*.

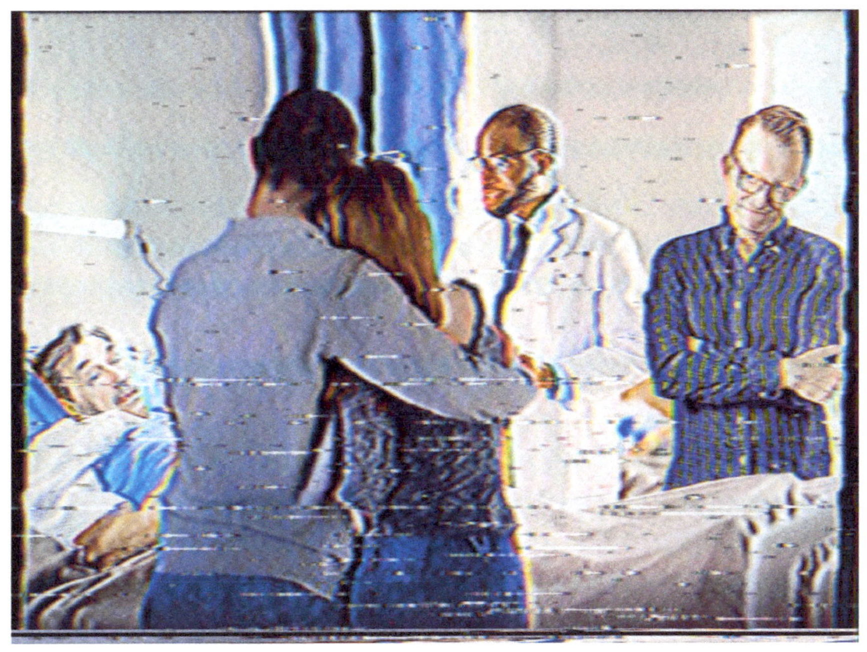

03:48:03   This is how we . . . love.

Some of the Characters
from *This Is How We Love*
and Their Fascinating
Backstories!

GEORGE

*The Black Gang
Banger*

It is not easy being a young black man in the United States of America in the 1990s.

Here is a perfect example: George the black gang banger, a gentle giant of a 22-year old who becomes involved in the life of the Adams family after a terrible car accident.

All humans, regardless of race or skin color or annoying personality traits, are capable of overcoming obstacles. And all men share at least a few things in common: in Bizz's and George's cases, their mutual love for baseball, earning boatloads of money, and gambling on computer-solitaire shirtless.

Although a mathematical genius, George B. White is forced to "sling" illegal drugs to support his large family, and while this particular career path might appear at first to be exciting and "tight," it is, in reality, a dangerous occupation that can only lead to death or a lifetime stuck in a government-subsidized wheelchair that barely functions and does not look "slick."

Faced with illegal drug-dealing or befriending a rich Caucasian family, George is fortunate enough to experience the latter. But he's not the only lucky person in this relationship: for it soon becomes clear that George is a genius when it comes to not only algebra but also solving board puzzles, a major plot point that brings the entire family together at the film's end as they wait somewhat impatiently for Bizz to die in an upscale hospital room.

Says Bruce R. Leigh, pharmacy manager at the Giant Grocery on Old Georgetown Road and the actor who portrayed this young black man: "I loved the script when they handed it to me. I was here in the grocery. I know the producer Mr. Walton from when he comes in here to shop. He's nothing but respectful. Mr. Walton is well aware I want to model, to act. In fact, I've done some special modeling for him. The character of George is about ten years younger than I am but I definitely know kids like that, they come into this store and try to shoplift wild-apple gum and other sweets and junk food they like. I'm not good at algebra, so *that* took some real acting! I am good at playing 'street.' George is an amazing character who I think will do much to change the racial tension in this country."

Tough on the outside, tender on the inside (much like a cheap cut of beef brisket), George is a character who will stay with you long after you find yourself weeping after hearing a line of dialogue that is sure to explode straight into the public's consciousness: "Yo! I guess *we all* just our own type of 'dawgs.'"

In the end, we are *all* "dawgs." Perhaps just of wildly different skin colors and tax brackets.

MATTHEW THE WRITER/DIRECTOR SAYS

. . .

"I wanted to create a minority character that your average American could abide, someone you'd look out your car window at and only want to lock the doors normally. In this case, if you wanted to take a longer look, you would like what you see. This is perhaps the most complicated character I ever created, with just so many layers. I researched all this by visiting street corners in some very 'tough' urban neighborhoods. The blacks I saw didn't seem all that different from me, except maybe when it came to their lingo and eating habits. So I got to wondering: What would happen if a rich person who was white and a poor person who was black crashed into each other with their cars? Would that be the only way they'd ever meet, these two from such vastly different worlds, one who once walked on the moon and the other who steps upon littered condom wrappers and other urban detritus on a daily basis? I thought it was the perfect 'Macmuffin' to explore some very tough racial matters that viewers might not think about otherwise. For that, I pat myself on my back. I hope this is just the start of more great works of art tackling 'racism' down the road."

BOBBY

The NASCAR Driver

It is not easy being the son a world-famous astronaut, especially with half your face burned off!

Bobby Adams has always had "the need for speed" in order to emulate the heroism displayed by his ultra-famous astronaut father, Bizz Adams. At the age of six, Bobby broke his arm trying to "land on a planet"—in reality, jumping from a Burger King roof onto a ficas bush.

But gaining the attention of his father has never been an easy feat. How does one impress a man who landed on the moon and then escaped a deep-space explosion caused by his own ignorance? In Bobby's case, he decides to achieve the prestigious title of world-class NASCAR Driver Sponsored By Mello Yello. Perhaps winning the World NASCAR Championship and representing a yummy soda brand could help his father love him once again?

During one such championship, in 1986, Bobby swerves to avoid a baby who has mysteriously crawled onto the track. The baby thankfully lives. But in the ensuing explosion, half of Bobby's face is sadly burned off. Taking to his bed, Bobby is looked after by his attractive wife Rachey who attempts to arouse him from his stupor with promises of "light sex." This doesn't work. Fearing that Bobby may never function as a normal again, Rachey does the only thing she feels might work: she hooks out as a high-class escort to earn enough money to hire a Beverly Hills surgeon to fix her husband's atypical looks. In an exciting twist, the surgeon is female.

On top of that, Rachey decides to adopt a grown Indian gentleman named Peckerwood—"Pecker" for short. Pecker's parents were killed years ago by a consortium of greedy white developers who ejected them from the makeshift encampment in the woods where they had lived deliciously free from modern society's bonds for decades.

At first, Bobby is against this somewhat unorthodox idea. He has enough on his plate, certainly, such as his disfigured face. Why should he also have to worry about an adopted Indian adult to raise? What good could this strange man from another culture possibly do for him? But all worries dissipate when Pecker saves the family's beloved blind dog, Bones, from beneath the local power lines during an exceedingly dangerous Los Angeles thunderstorm.

"This was not my first acting role," proclaims Josefe Ramirez, the actor who plays Bobby in *This Is How We Love*. "I had done a few productions at the Toby Dinner Theatre up in Olney. I also was in a movie from some guys at Montgomery College about an intelligent parrot owned by an epileptic go-go dancer. So what I loved about Bobby was that he, too, had a damaged face. Mine was burned after I fainted face-first into a bowl of Swedish meatballs at an Ikea cafeteria. So I wasn't really *acting* acting."

Stubborn, headstrong, and supremely proud, Bobby is not a character to be taken lightly. So much possibility still exists within this physically and emotionally mutilated human, and when we see him hover in a rented TV traffic helicopter above Brentwood at the end of our film, flown by the formerly homeless man Klat, we can all celebrate that Bobby has achieved, at long last, his lofty, majestic dream of finally becoming a real-estate agent in Brentwood, California!

It's a fine ending for a perfectly adequate man.

MATTHEW THE WRITER/DIRECTOR SAYS

. . .

"I wanted to create an ugly character everyone would care about, someone modern, not ringing a bell in a Parisian tower. I once passed a car driven by a beautiful woman, with a terribly disfigured man sitting there in the passenger seat, next to her, just as happy as you please. What was their story exactly? Was she his nurse? Was he rich and was she exceedingly poor? What in the hell was going on there?! Bobby is a complicated man, not helped by his relationship with his mother who drinks too much, his father who spends his days re-living his successes (and many failures) as an astronaut, his son who is a Grunge rock and roll singer and on illegal drugs, another son who is deaf and somewhat annoying. That's a shit sandwich. How does one eat a shit sandwich? I guess there are a few ways. Bobby eats it in pieces. Others would eat it whole. That's what I love about this character. The song Mike + the Mechanics wrote for the film called 'Shut Up and Fly (and Don't Crash Land)' encapsulates this character very well. Everyone has a bit of Bobby in them. Hopefully hidden down very deep and not visible."

AZURE ADAMS

It's been said many times but it's worth saying again:

There is no greater purpose for a woman than to become the wife of a world-famous astronaut and to then bask in that great man's fame and fortune!

Cliché alert, but true!

Imagine the glory that comes with such a role! Invitations to the White House! Fancy luncheons with other wives of astronauts! Riding in the back of a rented, American-made convertible in parades while your husband sits up front!

But what happens when all this glory ends? And a woman is then forced to confront her biggest fear: living with a formerly famous astronaut who's impotent because he killed so many people, including children, due to his own stupidity?

As with so many other women, Azure turns to pickling herself in the zesty juices that the Aztecs once called "Dream Water." You see, while gorgeous, Azure is an alcoholic, lonely within a huge compound, endless afternoons stretching before her, longing only for the touch of a man who still deems her worthy, a man capable of making love without the haunting thoughts of an exploding rocketship preventing him from achieving "liftoff" in the sexual male sense.

Enter the farm-strong Mexican gardener, Ray Ray, husband to Azure's long-time, loyal cook Angel. An absolute artist with shearing hedges, Ray Ray is also patient enough to understand that what Azure truly needs is maybe just someone to listen to her long enough for her to grow quiet and fall asleep in his wiry, brown arms.

Azure once had such high hopes for her future: a teenage debutante from Huntsville, Alabama, this Southern young lady on the go was the first female in her family to ever attend a university with the hopes of one day working as an executive assistant for a rich oil CEO. Choosing, instead, to marry a dashing young aviator before graduation, Azure made a decision that would come to haunt her later in life: even the young and the beautiful will one day grow old enough to become miserable, and once the inevitable occurs, there is little left to fill the void left by the absence of sexual congress.

Actress and Nu Skin salesperson Shannon Ferguson of Potomac, Maryland, says of the role: "Azure is all of us. Lonely, disappointed, sad, she adores her 3:00 P.M. drinky-poos. But what I saw in this character was the love for a man who is damaged by the decisions he made up in that sky. Her husband killed a lot of people, in space and on Earth, including children, but she never lost sight of the man beyond all that silliness. It was a fun movie!"

Brash, intelligent, and, most of all orgasmically frustrated, the alcoholic Azure yearns for a lost life that was once provided to her by her successful husband who's now sadly past his prime, physically as well as mentally and physically. Azure is a female character that *all* women of a certain age can happily relate to! Can you?!

MATTHEW THE WRITER/DIRECTOR SAYS

. . .

"Azure annoyed me to tears. I hated her. But that was a *good* thing. I figured if she was annoying to me, she'd annoy the audience, which I guess was her purpose. I hated everything about her. I wanted to murder her. And for her to be rejuvenated. And then to murder her again and again."

MELISSA ADAMS

Bizz and Azure's only daughter, Melissa, is a troubled woman in desperate need of a major makeover to become more physically attractive. That's not just in her head but obvious for everyone to see. It's just a very sad fact.

Melissa is also a depressive who stutters. Moreover, she is a lesbian. Her roommate Vicky Mantreo is a world-championship swing dancer whose boyfriend, Topper, is a skateboard and "blading" messenger who has accidentally stumbled upon a legal document that threatens the very existence of the entire Earth's rain forests. They make a dynamite team.

It's your typical modern 1990s young couple!

Melissa is a fan of the dark and broody style of "goth" music. Fully aware of her mother's slow-motion suicide, Melissa volunteers at a "suicide hotline," a job made only that much more challenging when her own stutter troublesomely comes into play and a few callers lamentably die or are paralyzed below the neck as a result.

Unlike her father, Melissa has no need for the spotlight. She is content to suffer in silence and has no greater dream than to teach advanced 8th grade algebra to a roomful of troubled inner-city colored students. When she first meets the gay, ethnic neighbor, Matthew Schwartzmann, they find they have much to talk about: cooking, baking, severe depression, thread counts in decorative doilies.

Purchasing a modern elocution course on compact disc, Melissa aims to change the directory of her life, and plans to work just one more night at the suicide hotline. Out of sheer chance, the very last call she receives is from her own mother! A funny thing happens! By talking her mother through her depression, Melissa miraculously cures her *own* depression, allowing her the freedom to teach mathematics and fall in love with the lesbian vice principal nicknamed "Butch."

Melissa represents so many young contemporary women of the early 1990s: a little lost, slightly disfigured and awfully hirsute, desperate for a life of happiness that has eluded her parents and now seems to elude her own "Generation X."   Drowning her sorrows by attending all-female rock festivals, such as the Lilith Fair or Woodstock

'94, Melissa does little to escape the true source of her *actual* problem: she is not as beautiful as her friends or neighbors. The makeover midway through the film helps but only to a degree: the tattered, fragile skin of a diseased peach is only capable of so much re-blossoming.

"But there's no quit in her," pronounces Becci Haverson of Potomac, Maryland, who plays Melissa in the film. "I had to dig real deep to act as someone so troubled, but she's not a person to just give up. I like that about her. I'm young myself, 22, and I know people like this: sulkers and downers and depressives. But they find a way to get up each morning and keep moving. That's important. You can't stagnate. For the stutter I spent an entire weekend with my uncle at Deep Creek Lake copying his mannerisms. It was a long, awful weekend but I got what I needed. My uncle later died steps away from his Filipino mail-order bride's hut."

Stronger than her debilitated appearance might ever suggest, Melissa is the perfect character for an entirely new generation to emulate: defiled but headstrong, never stopping until she reaches her final goal, no matter all of the more attractive women in her way. The goal? Not death, but, in Melissa's case, teaching kids no one else really wants very much to deal with.

MATTHEW THE WRITER/DIRECTOR SAYS

. . .

"If I ever had a daughter, she'd be Melissa. I never have and I never will. But I've often thought about who my daughter might be: a disaster but still with so much to offer. People might feel sorry for her but that's the wrong tact to take! My daughter would be intelligent and willing to help anyone, no matter their creed. For some reason, I always picture my imaginary daughter as a Mediocre Mary, like Melissa. Melissa is a good person and I hope the audience can sense that and rise above her other challenges—in my mind, the character dies happily in her forties, surrounded by her former black students who absolutely adore her. Maybe they killed her. I don't know."

FRITZ

The Nazi Guard

Not all Nazis are evil, as we delightfully witness in *This Is How We Love*'s most talked-about character, Fritz the Auschwitz Guard.

In a lovely flashback, Azure's mother, Mildred, falls in love with Fritz, a kind Nazi commando who tenderly hands her a single red rose each morning through the barbed wire at the death camp before tea and roll call. Beyond being a terrible romantic, Fritz loves nothing more than entertaining the prisoners after their long day in the fields by performing the magic tricks that he had once impishly taken from the body of a decapitated American soldier.

But, regrettably, the prisoners' joy in witnessing this daily enchantment is cut short when Fritz is murdered by Nazi leadership for being "too nice." It's a sad end to a difficult life. And sad for the prisoners, too. Admittedly, Auschwitz was never exactly a five-star hotel, but now it's suddenly just another heart-rending, dispiriting place.

The one bright hope is that Mildred falls pregnant just in time for the Russian advancement, only to later give birth on a bed of lice-riddled hay in an abandoned barn. Out of the womb sluices Azure, whose strange beginnings will be difficult to jibe with her later very American childhood.

Adult Azure, of course, has no idea she's one-half Nazi until she stumbles upon a diary hidden inside a wood firkin up in the attic within the Adams' family compound. Upset at first, Azure eventually comes to terms with the fact that her birth father was a Nazi and her mother secretly a Jew. Neither are perfect options, but there is little she can do besides drink.

"Fritz was a character I had so much hatred of at first," says Mitchell Saunglebaum of Bethesda, Maryland, and himself Jewish. "I just didn't trust him. Most of my family was murdered by Nazis back in World War II. But my job as an artist is to find the decency in *everyone*. What does Fritz have that other Nazis don't? I thought Matthew making him a fan of magic was brilliant. He'd be able to take away the prisoners' every day fears and worries, and into a wondrous world where *anything* can happen. When I was reading the shooting script, there was a very long scene that impressed me greatly: Fritz makes the entire death camp disappear through magic. Like David Copperfield did with the Statue of Liberty. That was cut, lamentably."

Born in the wrong time and place, Fritz appreciates and deeply craves seeing the broad smiles on the faces of death camp prisoners of *all* races and sexualities. Perhaps owing to his importance in *This Is How We Love,* Fritz has the most songs (five) out of all the characters in the film, including "Pulling Hope from a Hankie," a powerful R&B ballad performed alongside hit-making soul duo Ashford & Simpson, who play factory laborers as nonspeaking extras. It was a small and yet important detail, as hate knows *no* color nor religion.

Fritz the Auschwitz Guard is a character we *all* can adore!

MATTHEW THE WRITER/DIRECTOR SAYS

. . .

"The Holocaust has always disturbed me, as it has others, I guess. I thought, *C'mon, I can't be the only one!* My original idea was to write a script that would focus on an adorable, talking gerbil who lives inside a Jewish person's skull-cap (without that Jewish person's knowledge or consent). But then I expanded on this idea. What would it have been like to have been a Nazi . . . but a *gentle* Nazi? Forced to work at these horrible death camps against their own considerable, teutonic will? I couldn't imagine a richer character. But I had a problem at first: the movie takes place in the current day in Los Angeles. So how to make this work? A contemporary Nazi? I don't think so! *A flashback! Let's involve one of the character's parents!* The specific characteristics of Fritz came to me in a dream: I was actually a Jew in a death camp who befriended a nice Nazi who showed me his card tricks. When I awoke, I was very happy. I thought this same joy could be spread to all of the Holocaust victims who still might be out in the real world, living. My movie didn't make the Holocaust *not* happen, true, but there is no doubt in my mind that there are literally hundreds of survivors who are way less haunted by their memories because of it. I'd love to send each a VHS copy but I fear they wouldn't know how to work the machine. And they don't need the additional frustration. By the way, there was an original actor who played Fritz, but he looked too Jewish. Here are two shots of the original actor taken by the on-set photographer. I think you'll agree with me!"

255

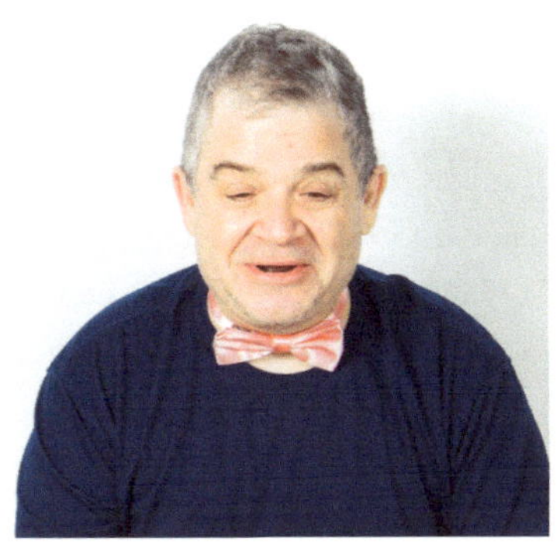

KLAT

The Homeless Man

Homeless but exceedingly wise, Klat is a gent with a *very* mysterious past!

How did this man come to be covered in suppurating sores? Did he ever have an occupation? And why is he sleeping at the bottom of the Adams' driveway on a thirsty X-rated beach towel, without shoes? It's a fascinating story.

The past few years have not been kind to Klat Larsen. Like so many others, Klat has a "drinking problem," meaning he drinks too much. But the reason he drinks too much comes down to a story so common among so many: while attempting to impress a beautiful, blonde Afrikaner by piloting a helicopter through a massive waterfall, Klat crashes the craft, the woman dies by drowning, and Klat is heroically saved by a group of shirtless, handsome South African male professional surfers. Klat returns to his job transporting illegal diamond smugglers back and forth to the mines, but it's just not the same.

One night, at a bar, Klat is asked if he'd like "a drink." He says yes … and his life is forever altered. Klat sinks into a world filled with booze and trouble, including a short stint in a South African prison. The crime? Murdering a rich tribal chief over a gorgeous woman singer who once sang backup on Paul Simon's classic African musical cassette, *Graceland*. Whilst in prison, Klat discovers the joys of the "written word" and teaches himself books on philosophy, history, religion, and how advanced alien intelligence might have been behind the invention of the fax machine. Emerging from this dangerous prison twelve years later a much more clever man, Klat heads back to the country in which he was born: the United States of America, upon which he immediately takes a job counseling the poor in Baltimore.

Fired for not having permission to counsel the poor in Baltimore, Klat begins to again drink. He thinks: *Why am I here? Am I worthless? Do I have something positive to provide? If so, how will I go about that? I have been through so many adventures in this lifetime. I have flown a helicopter into a beautiful waterfall so many times. Sure, one time it didn't work out for that one unfortunate, gorgeous woman! But it did, many, many times, for me! God she was beautiful!*

Taking a bus from Baltimore to Los Angeles, and then hitch-hiking over to the Brentwood neighborhood after hearing that the town's locals are liberal enough not to call the police on a homeless man on a beach towel, Klat arrives, by sheer chance and by good fortune, at the foot of the Adams' very long, winding driveway. At first, there is much confusion—between *both* Klat and the Adamses. Who is this man living in the driveway who has a Playboy insignia tattooed onto his forehead?

There's a simple answer: Bizz Adams comes to learn that while in prison, Klat was forced by the gang leader "Jeffe the Terrible" to have his forehead branded without his permission. The purpose of this act was to prove to Klat that you simply *cannot* treat women poorly. Feeling sorry for Klat and his infected forehead, Bizz strikes up a conversation … and he *likes* what he hears.

So does the rest of the family!

Having helped so many of the Adamses with their myriad problems, Klat the Homeless Man is invited into the family compound on Christmas Eve to celebrate their yearly festivity. He no longer must live at the foot of the family's driveway. Rather, Klat can now live in an unfurnished, barely-heated apartment above the garage that stores the family's Super-8 home vintage pornography movie collection. All that reading in prison did Klat a "world of good," and ultimately saved his life. He thus becomes an official member of the Adams family, here to provide support and wisdom and "brute force" and a "willingness to take out the trash in the pouring rain" whenever deemed necessary!

"His obnoxious drinking was my launching point into this awful character," says Eric Anderseen, proprietor of the Potomac, Maryland Paint & Hardware Store when not acting in big budget Hollywood movies. "Sad to say I have my own experiences with drink. Which is what I think Matthew saw in me for this role. There's a sadness with this character that just spoke to me. In my own life, I've never flown a helicopter, certainly not purposely straight into a waterfall, but I have done plenty of other silly things. For instance, I once ate a cat turd to impress a fellow student. I was in grad school in New Orleans. Klat has *so* much to offer. As for myself, I just played my own small part in bringing this magical, brilliant homeless man to life. Anyway, I have to go fix the paint-mixing machine now. And then get a drink."

Kind, loving, wise, a bit odorous, Klat may have once been homeless but he is never without *hope*. An inspiration to us all: alcoholic, homeless, or just temporarily shoeless.

MATTHEW THE WRITER/DIRECTOR SAYS

. . .

"This was a fun character to write, someone who is suffering terribly. It's based on someone I knew 'back in the day.' He was one of the smartest people I've ever known but he lived on a heating grate on the University of Ohio quad. Students would throw snack foods at him. Some would even wake him by blaring really loud stadium soccer horns next to his head. Everyone thought that was funny. It was but I wanted to know more. I invited him out for coffee. I was curious to see what he had to offer. He knew everything about everything. We became really good friends. I'd go to him whenever I had a problem of any sort and he could *always* solve it! In the movie, I left out the rash that ate away most of his limbs. I substituted that with the Playboy insignia forehead tattoo. The real-life Klat sadly died after a confrontation with an EPCOT Center security guard who had repeatedly warned him about setting up his makeshift tent a few feet from where visitors stood in line for *Captain EO*. I never did learn his real name. Benjy something? Lord, did he stink to high heaven!"

BIZZ ADAMS

At last we come to family matriarch Bizz Adams, former astronaut, American hero, subject of many books, television specials, and a 1969 hit parody song by the world-famous humorist Allan Sherman ("You Can't Bizz Your Buzz Back from the Byzantine Moon").

And yet Bizz's numerous woozy appearances on Johnny Carson's *Tonight Show* have now faded and this once heroic American character has entered middle-aged with a deep sense of guilt arising from his possible connection to murdering his colleagues and school children through his own incredible ineptitude.

Making matters worse, Bizz finds himself married to a woman, Azure, who is perhaps not as patient as she could be when it comes to his emotional and physical "issues." Frustrated with her husband's inability to perform in a sexual manner, Azure turns to the consistency of spicy love that only a brown-skinned Ray Ray seems capable of providing.

But Bizz is not a man to give up so easily—this is the very reason he became famous to begin with! Rearranging his thought process, retraining his sagging muscles through lifting water jugs filled with aquarium gravel, Bizz attempts to win back his wife, while also pushing back the annoyance he feels when forced to communicate in sign-language with his exasperatingly deaf grandson, Flatterhy.

Max Pearson, actor/orthodontist in Bethesda, Maryland, says about his role as the all-American astronaut that will be sure to launch him to stardom: "Space has always fascinated me. As has stardom. But what comes after? A lifetime of boredom? I'm lucky. If I ever do become famous and then less famous, I can always turn to my dental practice. What does Bizz have? What happens when all of the fame recedes? What's it like to kill people with your own stupidity? I've never killed anyone in the dentist's chair but I've come close. What's funny is that the one patient I almost killed is set to work on this film! I plan to give him a hug, although he has sued me successfully. I don't hold it against him. From what I hear, he can again chew his food without using his hands to move his jaws."

Handsome, still awe-inspiring, Bizz sets his lofty goals for the stars . . . even while finding that his "earthly problems" might be harder to solve than those that took place up in space, in an oxygen-drenched cockpit, with him lighting the celebratory cigar and killing his fellow astronauts.

It's an all-American glory story for the ages!

MATTHEW THE WRITER/DIRECTOR SAYS

. . .

"In many ways, the character who is closest to who I am as a person would have to be Bizz the Astronaut. I'm not saying I'm impotent—in fact, I proved quite virile on those occasions I was given the chance to prove myself—but I have done things that might have harmed people. How does one move on from that? Hopefully, with the same decency and dignity Bizz exhibited throughout his post-astronaut life. I also have many fears. I'm afraid of women who point with their pinkies. I hate blistered tomatoes on any starch. I have a very confident mien but beneath that strapping façade is someone with a few vulnerabilities. I have a terrible fear of any reptile who can give birth out of its mouth. The song 'What a Fool Believe' scares the shit out of me. When Bizz dies in the end, I cried when I wrote that. I was in the Hamburger Hamlet in the Valley. The waitress thought I was crying about the Sweet and Tender Fried Clams. I wasn't. Surrounded by family and friends, including the black gang member he met earlier in the film, Bizz makes one last connection with his deaf grandson. He makes a hand motion to turn on the morphine pump. I'm almost crying talking about it."

BONBON

The Parrot With HIV (left on cutting room floor)

MATTHEW THE WRITER/DIRECTOR SAYS

. . .

"I really tried to use *This Is How We Love* to not just entertain but also to say something *relevant* about the world. I wanted people to leave the theater laughing and crying but also to have their hearts and minds pumped up to eleven. HIV/AIDS is a big deal, of course, and I thought it might be fun and cinematic to tell the story of that dreaded disorder through a bird instead of an all-too-predictable human. It was a setback when a waitress at my favorite diner told me what the 'H' in HIV stood for. But I pushed past that. Bonbon was supposed to be Azure's pet, a source of (platonic, nonsexual) companionship to help her deal with her husband's many problems. She, in turn, would assist Bonbon to cope with his medical issues and the social stigma brought about by his unfortunate condition. We ultimately cut Bonbon from the shoot after he dragged one of the human babies born on-set (a two-pound preemie) back to his enclosure and attempted to feed her regurgitated nutrient crumbles. I just sent his stuffed corpse to the Smithsonian but it came back unopened."

262

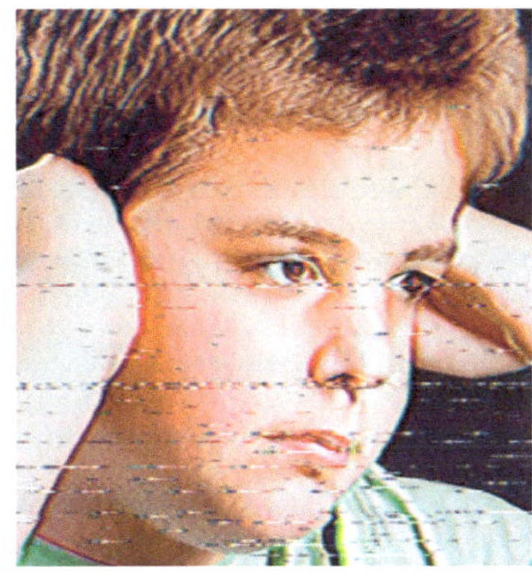

FRANKIE ADAMS

*Bizz Adams'
Imaginative Autistic
Son (left on cutting
room floor)*

MATTHEW THE WRITER/DIRECTOR SAYS

. . .

"I was enthralled by the beloved series finale to *St. Elsewhere* in which the entire universe of the show was revealed to exist solely in the intense imagination of the harebrained son of one of the blue-collar characters. I thought I could do a version of my own for *This Is How We Love* in which the very last scene featured Bizz coming home from work, not as a former astronaut who has to get past his guilt/impotence for all the people he slaughtered, but as someone who digs ditches. He sees Frankie, pats him on the head, and says, 'I wish I knew what was going on inside that Rain Man noggin of yours.' Then we see Frankie has been playing with action figures, but they all correspond to characters from the movie, except for the characters I cut, obviously. Ultimately, I worried people would accuse me of ripping off someone else's iconic idea, so I nixed it and felt bad for keeping this retarded actor out of school for nine weeks."

LIZZ
AND RYAN
CROSSINGTON

(left on cutting room floor)

MATTHEW THE WRITER/DIRECTOR SAYS

. . .

"This was by far the biggest disappointment—one of many, anyway—in the entire production. The Crossingtons were a couple I wrote for the film, and we shot this scene, and it was incredibly powerful. But in the end, we chose to cut; in a film packed with quality, you have to make a few agonizing decisions. The Crossingtons, Lizz and Ryan, were the parents of Topper. Both were climate scientists working for the Environmental Protection Agency. Sadly, Ryan is forced to sacrifice his penis in order to escape the primitive Brazilian tribe deep in the Amazon rainforest. Isn't that terrific? The actors who played these scientist characters were themselves a married couple that attended the same church as James Walton. I hope no moviemaker steals these characters and the overall idea! There was also a subplot about a guy turning forty. Isn't that clever? I'm going to make some future filmmaker a multimillionaire and a hero to critics, so you're welcome in advance, whoever you are! Maybe the guy's even a *virgin*, I don't know. I'm just *giving* away my ideas now!"

"I really thought the best thing to do," says the character of Ryan Crossington, "was to head on down to the Amazon and attempt to make contact with a colored tribe who've never spoken before to anyone who is white. Looking back, perhaps we should have maybe stayed in Arlington, Virginia?"

Ryan comforts Lizz on the fourth day of not having a penis: "Just give it a couple more weeks to get used to, hon. And don't worry about me. I barely even notice. Anyway, here's your gift. The simple tribesmen made it for us. Wasn't that nice? They're very handy. It's a genuine mahogany wood cock."

Ryan puzzles over a proposition for Lizz: "They gave us this totem before they chopped my penis off? *Hmmm*, I have an idea. Pull down your trousers, hon …"

Lizz rejects Ryan's strange new attempts at intimacy: "You want *me* to use this on my *own* damn self?!"

"I've been getting along just fine. You no longer have to worry about satisfying *my* needs," Lizz says, revealing her rudimentary, yet effective bedroom aid talisman. In the next scene, sadly, we learn that this most primitive dildo tends to put a curse on any vagina upon that which it comes into contact. In celebration, the Brazilian villagers frolic about in jaunty brightly-feather-bespoked glory!

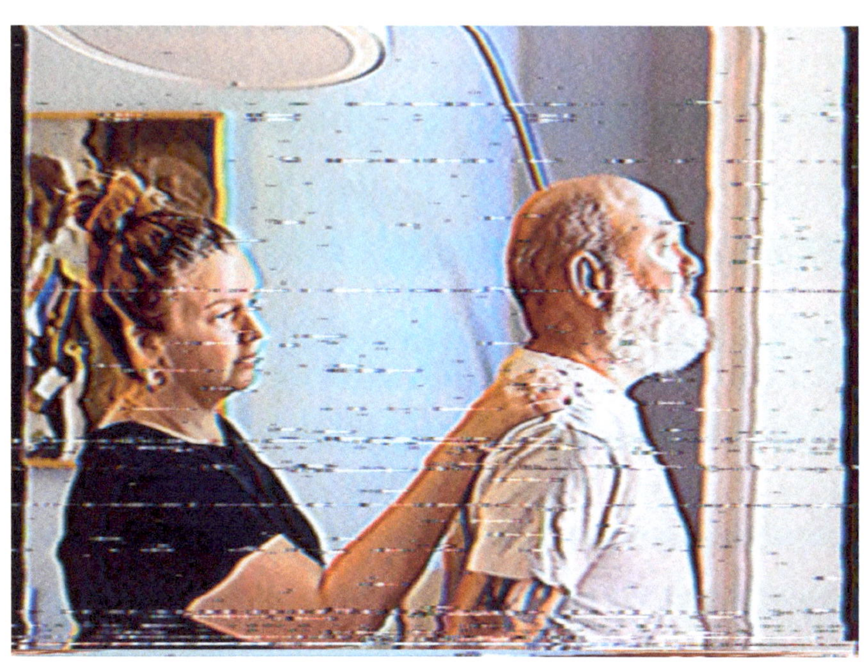

"I honestly can't believe that I'm forty!"
 "I know! I can't believe it either! Forty! Imagine!!"
"It's insane! Forty!"
"I think of myself as so young! But forty!"
"Wow."
"Yeah!"
"Forty!"
"Incredible!"
"Sad."
"Forty."

Famous Quotes

from *This Is How We Love*!

GEORGE THE BLACK GANGBANGER: "You're a real tough woodchuck, huh?"

VICKY ABOUT BOYFRIEND TOPPER: "Knowing him, the suicide note would be written in Dunkin' Donuts font!"

BIZZ TO THE BLACK GANG BANGER [next to the house's in-ground pool]: "I remember you! We formed an instant disconnection!"

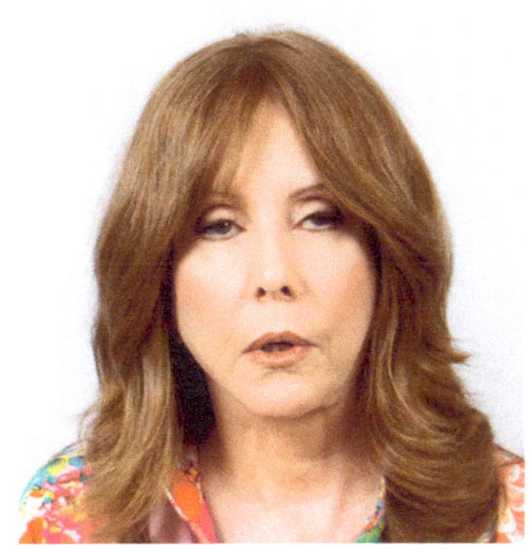

AZURE ON BIZZ'S ADORATION FOR HIS DAUGHTER MELISSA: "Does he *love* her! He *adores* her! He practically cut her umbilical cord with a pair of ceremonial ribbon-cutting scissors!!"

BOBBY TO HIS TWO SONS, TIMMY AND FLATTERHY: "Oh, if it isn't Leopold and Low-Brow!"

AZURE TO BIZZ AT THE HOLLYWOOD SIGN: "Give him the Spanish Archer, Bizz! The El-*Bow*!"

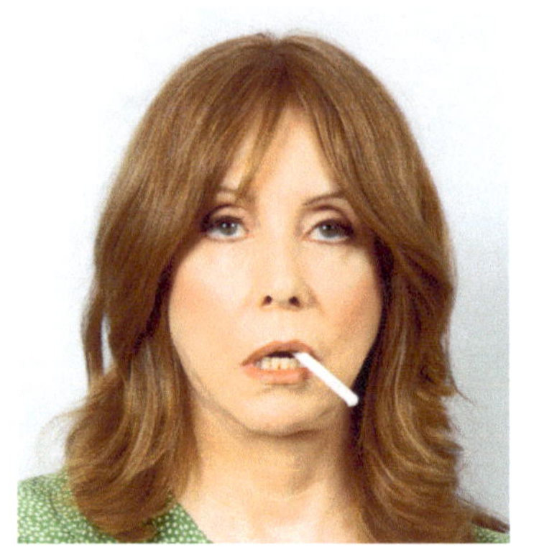

AZURE TO BOBBY AND FLATTHERY: "Look at you two! Joined at the *unhip*!"

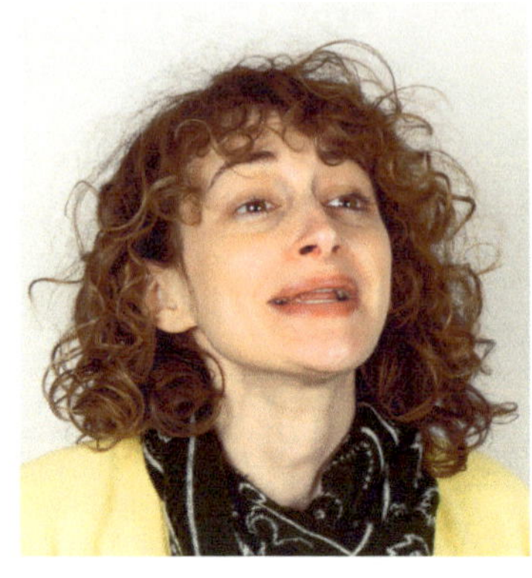

MELISSA ADAMS TO BOSS AND LESBIAN LOVER [at the playground]: "I am an ignorant Japanese schoolgirl. *Teach* me."

GEORGE THE BLACK GANG BANGER TO FORMER ASTRONAUT BIZZ: "You put the laughter in 'manslaughter'!"

NAZI GUARD FRITZ TO
HIS COMMANDER, ROLF:
"From the shoulders up, nothing's
happening. From the kneecaps
down . . . nothin' happening.
But between the courthouse and
the fire station, the show is right
there!"

MARCUS'S MOTHER TO
RANDY FRIEND GAYLE [in
the Station-to-Station Dance
Club]: "I just wanna . . . straddle
a mechanical mustache!"

MELISSA ADAMS TO
SUICIDE RISK ON
TELEPHONE HOTLINE:
"Trust me! I own an elocution
course on compact disc!"

VICKY TO BIKE MESSENGER BOYFRIEND TOPPER: "I come from the school of hard *cocks*, baby boy!"

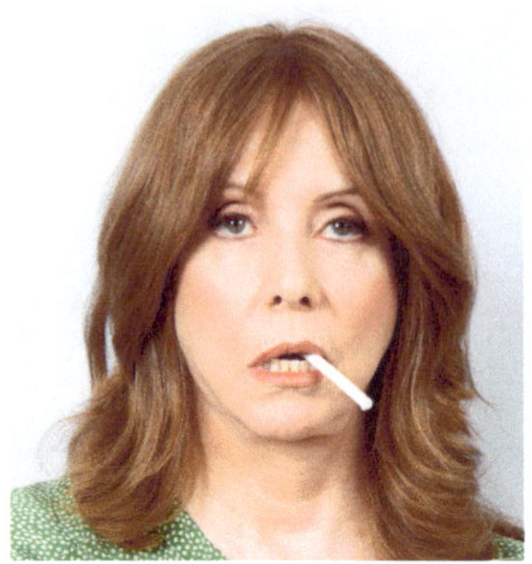

AZURE TO BRONZE-TONED RAY RAY, WHILE IN HIS ARMS, IN HIS BED, WITH HIM IN HER: "I like you. You fill every day with 'yay'."

KLAT THE HOMELESS MAN TO FORMER ASTRONAUT BIZZ: "You oughta slack *back*, Jack!"

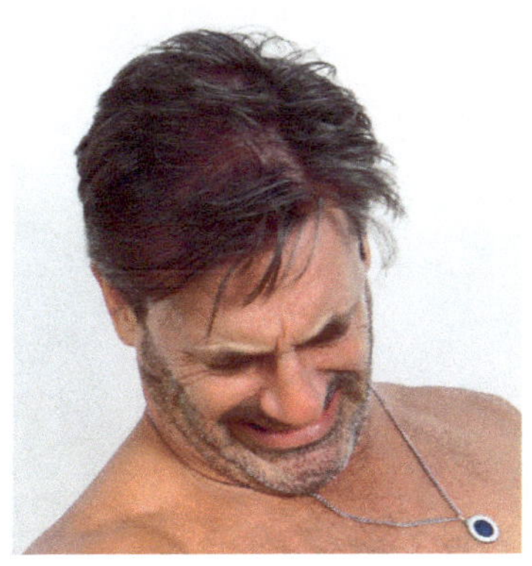

BIZZ TO ASTRONAUT GROUPIE, BARBI: "My awareness muscle is fully honed, boned and ready to get groaned!"

ANGEL TO SELF: "Your mother gave birth to you through her asshole, together with a pile of shit, while lightning flashed!"

LESBIAN VICE PRINCIPAL TO BIZZ [after their excursion to Joshua Tree]: "This gas-station blowfish . . . it ain't sittin' so pretty, daddy."

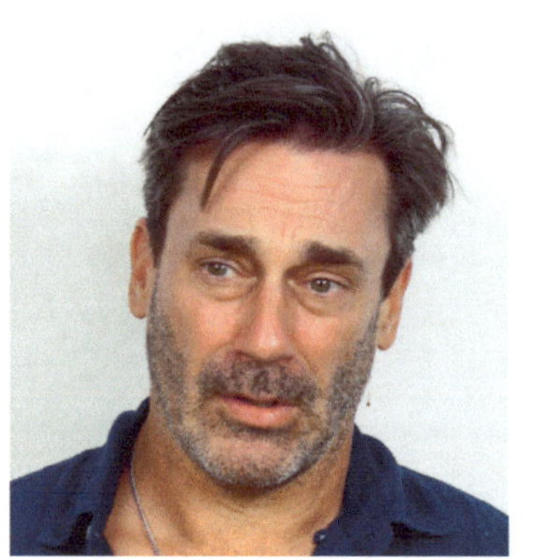

BIZZ TO AZURE [about his six-week disappearance]: "Where was I? Oh yeah. Relieving myself of my greater and lesser needs."

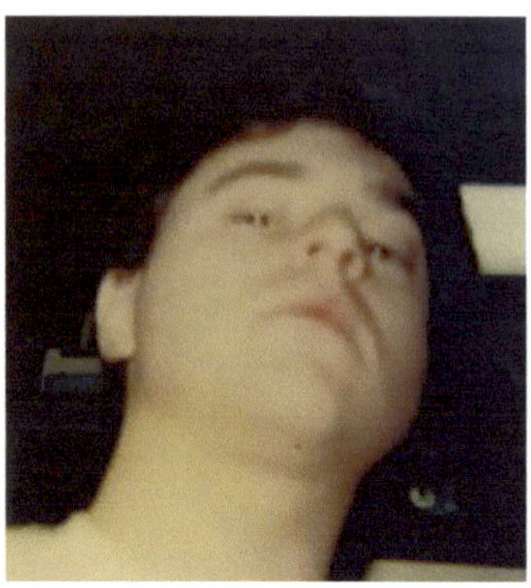

MALE NURSE ABOUT BIZZ, POST SURGERY [hospital hallway]: "His post-surgery breath! It's off the charts!"

VICKY TO ROOMMATE MELISSA: "Once you go Persian, there ain't no other version!"

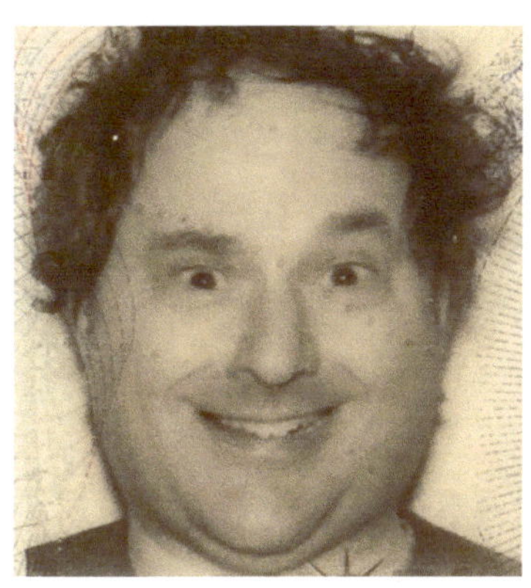

JEFFE THE TERRIBLE,
SOUTH AFRICAN PRISON
[flashback]: "Blood on my knife
or shit on my dick, I *will* collect
what I am owed!"

Cast Trivia!

ACTOR ROBERT McGULLIGAN

*"Topper Crossington,
Gen-X Blader"*

Robert—or "Bobbsy" to his friends—is the product of a show-biz family, his father having worked one summer as a "human chew toy" at The Big Gasp Circus outside Reno, Nevada, and his mother as an assistant tailor on the 1983 Washington D.C. National Theatre production of *Barnum!*

Robert's favorite actor is Paul Reiser, but only his role in *Mad About You*

Robert is unable to ride a skateboard in real life

Robert's first acting role was "boy in red striped shirt" on the 1981 television advertisement for Alexandria, Virginia's Mattress Discounters

Robert refuses to drink diet soda, no matter the peer pressure

Robert performed all his own stunts on *This Is How We Love,* minus the enormously dangerous skateboarding scenes

Robert's favorite VHS rental store is "That's Rent-ertainment" in Potomac Village

As for the future, Robert wants to continue to act: "I plan to do this for the rest of my life. Not making it is *not* an option!!!!"

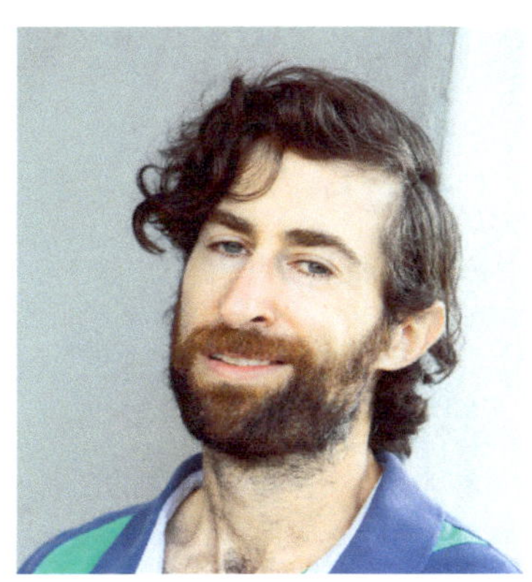

ACTOR RANDY SONDENDFELD

"Matthew, Gay Jewish Neighbor"

Randy is not "gay" but he is Jewish

Randy's favorite on-set story concerns Bones the "Blind Dog" stealing a mouthful of soiled surgical gauze from the nurse's tent

When not acting in major Hollywood productions, Randy likes to "hacky sack" with his "best bros," although he does not "love it"

Randy worked for ten years as a bagger at the Giant Grocery on Old Georgetown Road and was named Employee of the Month twice, which Randy humbly dismisses as some kind of "charity BS"

Like the character of "Manuel" in *This Is How We Love,* Randy's mother, with whom he does not have a close relationship, struggles with schizophrenia

Randy has a crush on Melinda McGraw who plays former FBI agent Cydavia 'Cyd' Madison on *The Commish*

As for the future, Randy would like nothing more than to continue to act: "This is it for me! I can't go back to retail. It's this or nothing. But I will make it! Not making it is *not* an option!"

ACTRESS JENNIFER McMURPHY

"Angel, Wife of Hispanic"

Jennifer adores tacos and fried plantains. This is why she is often confused for being Hispanic, though she assures us that she is "most definitely not, believe me."

Jennifer was originally up for the role of Azure, Bizz's wife, but appeared too ethnic. No amount of blanching makeup could remedy this.

Jennifer's favorite fruit is the tomato (yes, it's a *fruit*, yo!)

In the movie's romantic scene that takes place in the garden's shed, Jennifer cried for real

Jennifer is currently auditioning for a speaking role in the Hollywood big-budget production biopic of the very popular rap group The Fat Boys. She will settle for nonspeaking extra, however. She just wants to be part of this incredibly special moment!

Jennifer has no intention of ever stopping acting: "There's *no* other option! This is it for me! I'm going to become successful! I *know* it!"

ACTOR LEO CAPITALIANO

"Manuel, Schizophrenic"

Leo is the second cousin of CIA director James Woolsey

Once on vacation in Aruba, Leo was hospitalized for food poisoning

Leo owns an 8-year-old female bulldog named "Hugey Lewis"

Leo's favorite movie is *Indiana Jones and the Temple of Doom*. His least favorite? The one where the two men sit in a restaurant and "just talk."

Although not schizophrenic himself, Leo has great respect for those suffering from the disease's many insidious effects

In order to play Manuel the Schizophrenic, Leo paid a day visit to Saint Elizabeth's Hospital in Washington D.C. When Leo mentioned he was performing in a movie, he was assigned his very own schizophrenic.

Leo would love nothing more than to continue to act: "This is it for me, truly. I really can't do anything else. It's this or play guitar in a rock band. I will make it or die trying!"

ACTOR
KERMAN GOTZ

"Flatterhy The Deaf Boy"

Although not deaf in real life, Kerman has great respect for the hearing-compared community and what burdens they must live through on a daily, frustrating basis

Kerman's very first movie role was Jebediah in *Children of the Corn II: The Final Sacrifice,* shot entirely just south of Virginia Beach, Virginia

Kerman's all-time favorite book is the abbreviated version of James Michener's "Hawaii"

Kerman's favorite actor is the exceedingly funny Dom DeLuise. While not himself obese, Kerman adores how Mr. DeLuise refuses to allow his weight to interfere with the laughter.

Kerman's current haircut is based on the bangs made popular by DJ on *Full House*

Kerman is an accomplished cardboard "brick" juggler

When not on set, Kerman favors ripped jeans, casual T-shirts from the Gap, and leather vests. He says the outfit makes him look a bit like a "desperado"—but in a good way!

Kerman claims the insecurity of being unemployed as an actor does *not* frighten him: "I wouldn't know what else to do! *This* is it. I *have* to make it. There is no other choice for me! *Onward to fame*!!!"

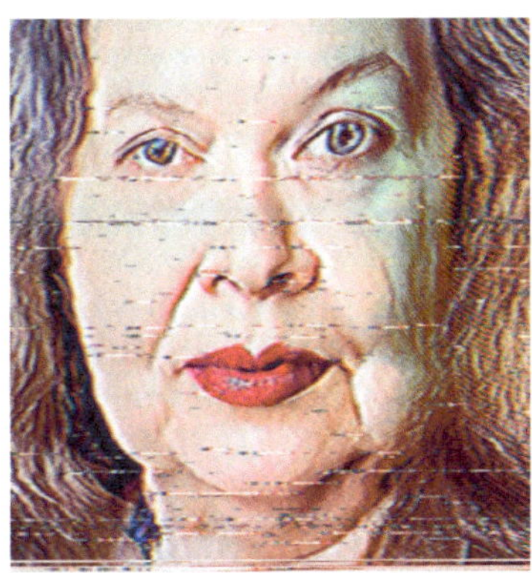

ACTRESS
KATHRYN KARIS

"Mother of Azure, Nazi Lover"

Kathryn was "discovered" at the age of four while eating a plate of silver-dollar pancakes at the Silver Spring Diner in Silver Spring, Maryland

Kathryn plans to keep in touch with *all* of the cast members from *This Is How We Love,* even the actors who play the disrespectful Nazi Auschwitz guards. They're *nice* guys in real life. It all comes down to incredible acting!

Kathryn's least favorite holiday is Thanksgiving. Easter was once her favorite. For personal reasons, she now has none.

Kathryn is not comfortable with the press and refuses to give interviews

Kathryn's favorite saying is: "If you lick my heart, you'd die from the poison"

Kathryn made the "blooper reel" more than any other actor or actress on *This Is How We Love,* more than 62 times! That's why she was nicknamed "Kathryn Screw It All Up"!

Kathryn has taught herself how to sign her name in hieroglyphics

Kathryn will continue to act because: "What else will I do? This is it for me. I *have* to act! I can't do anything else! There is no other choice for me! It's this or *nothing*!!"

ACTOR
LANNY ADIL

"Timmy the Grunger"

Lanny is five foot eight inches but looks much shorter

Lanny's father, Tom, is a very successful investment counselor for Potomac Millionaire Ventures in the Digeo Building just behind the Montrose Road California Pizza Kitchen

Lanny has written his own movie script. It's a cross-country buddy movie with a twist. One character is white. The other black. Both are prepping for a colonoscopy.

On the set of *This Is How We Love,* Lanny was famous for his pun-filled jokes. The laughter these received was the sole reason he was kept in the cast even after a series of "inappropriate" inner-calf rubs.

In real life, Lanny's favorite "alternative" group is 4 Non Blondes. He has seen them perform 27 times.

For the scene featuring rock and roll singer, Kenny Loggins, Lanny *really* was enjoying the show and not just pretending!

Lanny plans to continue to act: "This is no hobby for me. I've given everything I have to make this a career. It's this or nothing. There is no other choice for me! God help me if this doesn't work out! I mean it! I'll kill myself! Or *others!*"

ACTRESS LUISA STENHENHET

"Vice Principal, Lesbian"

Luisa is not a lesbian in real life but has a sister who is a "bisexual"

Luisa is deathly afraid of helicopters and carefully avoided the *This Is How We Love* set on the day that the helicopter crash was planned but not (ironically) on the day it actually occurred

When not working as an actress on major Hollywood movie productions, Luisa works as a volunteer at the Seven Locks Preschool on Seven Locks Road

Luisa has a phobia of "soft cheese" and mountain lions

Luisa was one of the six actresses on *This Is How We Love* to give birth on set, inside makeup trailer #2. Labor lasted sixteen hours but she was helpfully provided with a bottle of foundation to bite down upon during contractions.

Continuing to act into her "golden years," Luisa opines: "I wouldn't know what else to do with myself. This is what I was born to do. I was born to act. It's this or nothing. *There is no other choice for me!"*

ACTOR IVAN "REX" ALEXANDER

"Marcus the White Thief"

As a child, Ivan did not want to become an actor. He wanted to become a veterinarian specializing in marsupials. For unspoken reasons, however, this opinion darkened considerably after college, and he changed his mind.

Ivan is a firm believer in the "method" style of acting and because of that, he stole from his castmates throughout the making of this film (he *did* return everything!!)

Ivan is currently up for the part of "Tino the white postal worker" in the forthcoming hit WB sitcom *Brotherly Love*

Ivan's younger brother, Marco, is the account manager for Trevor, one of the members of the extremely popular "Boy Band" Puss-Ville

Ivan plans to move to Hollywood this spring: "This is my big chance but I *won't* mess it up. I've wanted to act forever. I plan on acting until I die. There is no other choice. This is *it* for me. I *have* to succeed!"

ACTOR JOE ROSE

*"Peckerwood the Adopted
Indian Adult"*

Although not an Indian in real life, Joe very much respects the magical traditions the Indians have passed down for literally decades.

In the "Rescuing Bones the Blind Dog" scene, Joe's nasty trip and fall and his fracturing of his femur was a "blooper" but kept in the movie regardless. The majority of laughter from cast and crew was removed by editors.

During the shooting of *This Is How We Love,* Joe memorized the Navajo phrase for "Won't you take me to the closest restaurant?"

Joe attended high school with Jussie Smollett, the future star of Fox's very popular sitcom *On Our Own*

Joe plans to act forever: "There's nothing I love more. I can't see myself doing anything else. Acting brings me the greatest joy. I won't quit. I will *never* quit. This is *it* for me! *It's this or die!!!*"

CHARLIE BOY

"Bones the Blind Dog"

Before being run over and killed by an actress from *Boy Meets World* on the 405 highway, Charlie Boy was trained to humorously slap one paw over his right eye as if not wanting to see something embarrassing, such as an elderly nude woman prancing before him

Charlie Boy was born in Alhambra, California, and is thought to be a direct descendant of the original "1977 Litter of Pups" famed music producer Phil Spector let run wild on his extensive Malibu property

The trainer for Charlie Boy, James Emera, also trained Barbra Streisand's toy poodle, Nosh, in the hit 1976 movie *A Star is Born*. Nosh would bark loudly every time Kris Kristofferson's character would groom his beard with his thumbs!

Charlie Boy's all-time favorite snack was a paper bowl of off-brand BacoBits purchased from any Dollar Store

Charlie Boy was born with his pancreas on the *outside* but was surgically "fixed" by an El Salvadoran veterinarian student before entering the acting profession

Before being run over and killed by an actress from *Boy Meets World* on the 405 highway, Charlie Boy wanted nothing more than to continue his very successful career as a canine actor . . . and yet now finds himself buried next to the baby skunk who played Michael Jackson's best friend, "Gunnar," in the hit 1977 musical *The Wiz*

This Is How We Rub

THE 1996 PORN PARODY OF *THIS IS HOW WE LOVE*

(Excerpted from *Porn Parodies Movie Dictionary*,
2004 Liberty Publishing. Used with Permission of the Author)

PLOT:

Written, directed, and produced by one Chuck Dayton, *This Is How We Rub* is the bizarre, unintentionally hilarious porn parody of the 1994 critically loathed *This Is How We Love*. Former astronaut Jizz Adams, 24, lives in a 1,000 square foot one-bedroom Venice Beach condo. Haunted by a mishap in space (whacking off), Jizz is bored by the drudgery of having to fuck his gorgeous 22-year-old wife, Cherri. Into this quaint picture steps a dazzling Mexican-American maid, known around Los Angeles as "Spicy Lil Firecracker." While Cherri is off to work as a massage therapist, Jizz and Senorita fuck beside an above-ground pool with a thin skim of grease atop it. Stumbling upon this delicious scene is a wisecracking homeless man named Butt Krack. As he joins in the festivities, we learn of Butt Krack's backstory through woozy flashback: once a hang-gliding instructor in Malibu, he'd earn extra money by ferrying wine spritzers to the female co-eds at Pepperdine. He's known for his famous line to any and all ladies, no matter their looks: "What troubles you, my pet?" Sadly, one falls to her death while strapped into his hang-glider. The reason? They were fucking too hard.

Sprinkled into this boiling, herpetic concoction are an endless parade of horny characters, all weaving and screwing their way through each others' stilted lives: an adopted, fully-grown virgin named Bullfrog; Bullfrog's sister, Bullshit, the owner of a high-end sex-toy emporium in Brentwood; quarterback Robbie Hostetleir of the Denver Broncos (joking; just a guy dressed as a generic football player); Spray Spray, a "Horny-American" gardener who tends to the "bushes" at the apartment complex; a lesbian substitute teacher at the local masturbation clinic; Slopper, a Gen-X skateboard messenger who stumbles upon a secret, powerful legal document that might just solve the worldwide G-spot issue "once and for all"; and a plumber with three distinct, schizophrenic personalities: one who loves to fuck, one who hates to fuck, and one who could go either way. His name is A. Harry Rod.

Avoid.

RATING: *1 Semi-Erect Cock-A-Doodle-Don't*

CREDITS:

"A Chuck Dayton Production"

Screenplay: Chuck Dayton

Director: Chuck Dayton

Producer: Chuck Dayton

Shoot Location: 2229 Frey Avenue, Venice, CA

Shoot Duration: Three Days

Music: Music by DeLore

Release Date: July 31, 1996

CAST:

Jizz Adams: Tom Gainsborough

Cherri Adams: Remmy Democracy

Spicy Lil Firecracker: Deborah Lane

Butt Krack: Hunt Club

Pepperdine Student: Jenni Cook

Bullfrog the Virgin: Fox Runn

Bullshit: Hurdle Hills

Football Player: Jonny Falls

Horny-American Gardener: Jack Jack McGaff

Masturbation Clinic Substitute Teacher: Ridge Mist

Harry Rod the Plumber: Belz Milz

Armless Woman with Feathered Earrings: Sara Chocolate Soda

Youth at Soda Fountain: Sara Chocolate Soda (uncredited)

ABOUT PRODUCER/DIRECTOR/WRITER CHUCK DAYTON:

Here at the editorial offices of *Porn Parodies Movie Dictionary*, we very much like (and *need*!) to know the creative faces behind our most beloved, delicious fucking and sucking *mastur*-pieces. In all of our years here in our Pittsburgh, PA headquarters (since 1976) we have yet to *not* record what a porn parody creator looks like. We're proud to tell you that we have kept our streak alive— *barely*. Chuck Dayton apparently does not like to have his photo taken. He lives in New York City. Photographed by the always resourceful and lovely Miss Samantha Jay. More to cum in our next edition!

"To Be Honest? We Fucking Hated Each Other!"

The Complicated Working Relationship Between Lead Actor and Director

SPECIAL FOR THE 30TH ANNIVERSARY BOOK TIE-IN EDITION

By Maurice DeWitt

Much has been written over the decades about the disagreements between film directors and their lead actors and actresses: Burt Reynolds was no fan of Paul Thomas Anderson during the making of 1997's *Boogie Nights*. Hitchcock joked that his actors were no better than "cattle," and rumors of skirmishes between Hitch and Grace Kelly abounded on the set of 1954's *Rear Window*.

Add to this list the problematical relationship between actor Max Pearson and director and writer Matthew Michaud on the set of *This Is How We Love*. Frequent screaming matches would often nearly come to physical blows. Arguments over word choice, hand movements, facial expressions; even the preference for a brand of sunglasses would set one or the other off, delaying the shoot, frustrating those on set who would have loved to have been able to leave for home rather than listen to a three-hour verbal duel of "Vuarnet versus Ray Ban."

And yet there have never been any on-set evidence (audio, video, otherwise) of any of the numerous reported tussles—until now.

What follows are a series of stills from a behind-the-scenes VHS video taken on the afternoon of November 3, 1992, during the infamous "Lighting a Cigar to Celebrate the Moon Landing" scene, all 175 separate takes. The detailed descriptions come from Dr. Max Pearson and his wife, Dani, and no images may be used without permission of either.

DANI: "They hated each other. Always arguing, bickering. I took a VHS camera to the set on this day. It's a legendary fight but we never released the footage. They'd scream and then they'd take a break to scream some more. Max wanted to shoot the entire scene nude. He was always very proud of his body. Matty disagreed."

MAX: "I thought it'd be more interesting if my character were to be vulnerable. I *still* think I'm right. As an orthodontist, I never get to show patients my body. I wanted to remedy that and to use this as an excuse. I've been told by friends and patients that I have a fabulous body—or used to!"

DANI: "Remember how Matthew wanted you to have a 'droopy loopy eye'?"

MAX: "We were about sixty days beyond the point of me having promised my patients I'd be returning to my practice. I told Matt, 'No top dentist has droopy eye. Nor, for that matter, astronaut.' And then I said: 'If I'm not there slinging braces, guess what? Those teeth are gonna walk themselves over to the Dental Emporium across the street!' He didn't care."

DANI: "He wanted you to have an obstacle to overcome. He said, 'Without a handicap, you're just another schmuck standing around in a spacesuit full of piss.'"

MAX: "I still have no idea what that means."

DANI: "About 25 minutes in. Still arguing."

MAX: "At this point, we began to quarrel over what I'd say just before the spaceship blew. We had something like 'To a better future,' which I thought was fruity. I suggested something stronger: 'And what can go wrong *now?*' or 'Here's to a violent-*free* future' and then KABLAMO! *Irony*. Powerful."

DANI: "And he still wanted the droopy eye."

MAX: "He says, 'You ever heard of tape night, Max? Tape night is where the entire cell block tapes their tight fists with electrical tape and then fights their way back to their cells. The guards place bets on who sleeps in a bunk and who sleeps in a morgue. The point is, *If I can survive tape night, you can most surely survive redoing your scenes with a droopy eyelid.*"

MAX: "I took off my shoes. I remember one of the interns asking if I needed flip-flops. No, I didn't need flip-flops. I was just getting warmed up."

DANI: "About 45 minutes into the fight, here we are."

MAX: "He moved on from the droopy eyeball. He now wanted me to limp. But there's no fucking *limping* in space! Zero gravity makes that an impossibility!"

DANI: "Still arguing over what to say just before the rocketship explodes."

MAX: "He was saying *nothing* needed to be said. Okay, I thought. Maybe nothing needs to be said. So how about doing something *interesting*. Like 'shooting' Earth with my fingers? Shrugging as if to say, *They didn't teach this in the military, but so what?* I myself have never been in the military. Or NASA. I don't believe in aggressiveness. But I have a lot of friends in the Army. So I was thinking about something fun that the audience could really latch onto. Winking maybe?"

DANI: "'What is it you don't understand?' Max is asking here. 'No astronaut has ever eaten a fully-loaded hot dog in space to celebrate? *C'mon!*'"

MAX: "It just seems that the astronauts would take something very special up into orbit to eat when they did something cool. I thought a hot dog could be *super* fun."

MAX: "'Then how about a *mini* hot dog?'" I'm asking. I had a patient who worked at the Deli Den in the Cabin John Shopping Center. I was saying to Matt, 'Listen, I can get these for *free*. I can have them overnighted here! If it's a money issue, I'd even pay for them *myself*! I mean, how fun would it be for a spray of relish or a hot stream of mustard to be flying through the air?!' Matt said no. This was his baby."

DANI: "But didn't you later bring mini hot dogs onto the set and eat em anyway?"

MAX: "I did! Yeah! Into the mockup of a rocket ship cockpit. And I bit into one during take 45 or something. [Laughing] He was *not* happy."

MAX: "We both knew this was a big, big scene. Maybe the *key* scene in the entire flick. The reason for *everything*: for Bizz's failing relationships with his idiot kids; his sex problems with his floomy wife; his depression. All of it. It was my thought that Bizz had to be *extra* vulnerable here. So no hot dogs, fine. So maybe just take off my spacesuit and let my cock out for a little space-walk? I thought it was a gutsy acting choice."

DANI: "Max's ideas were coming fast and furious by now."

MAX: "Yeah."

DANI: "The cocaine helped."

MAX: "And being lit on Dexedrine. That's right."

MAX: "I might have been a little *too* forceful. Matthew turned against not just me, [but] my entire acting style. 'Too over the top.' 'Not *believable*.' 'Want someone like Nicholson.' Fine. But guess what? I'm *me*, not anyone else, certainly not Jack Nicholson. This is how I act. I do dramatic. Playing to the back row. That's what I do at my dental practice. The patients *love* it. Why wouldn't the movie audience?!"

MAX: "He was all like (mimicking, high voice): '*You have to do what I'm telling you! This movie has been living in my head for years!* This is what I *envisioned*! *You can't muck it up with hot dogs!*' (back to normal voice) And I was like, 'It doesn't have to be hot dogs in space! It can be *anything*! I mean, whatever … a Pop-Tart! I just want to make it fun for the audience, to get them *comfortable*, and then … KABLAMO!!"

DANI: "He told you to fuck off."

MAX: "He did, yes."

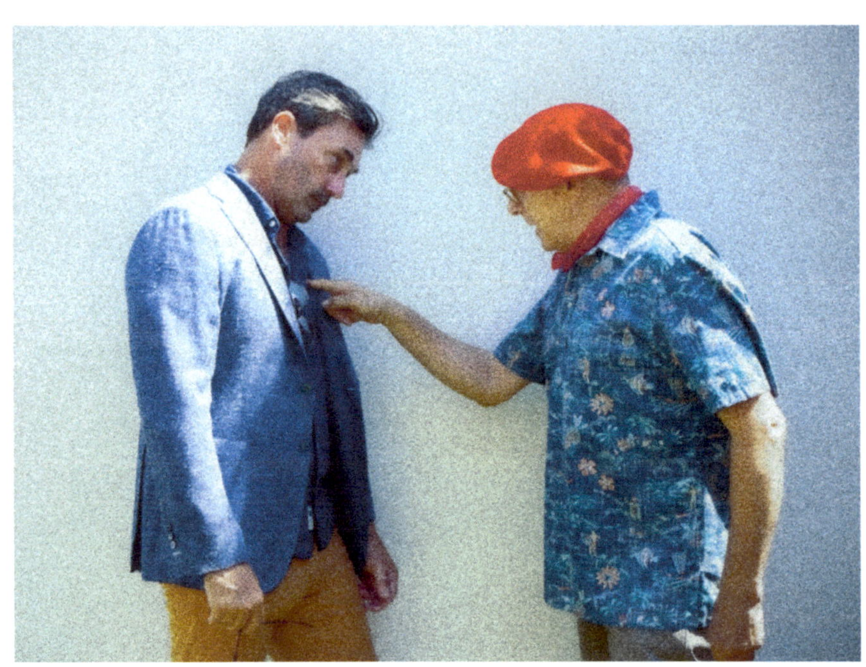

MAX: "So I said, '*Fine*. What would you *rather* me do? Just smile and light up a celebratory cigar? If that's what you want, *sure*, I'll do it! It's *no* problem! I don't have to be nude! This is your movie, not mine, right?' I was being sarcastic."

DANI: "He wasn't terrific at understanding sarcasm."

MAX: "No. We continued fighting for hours. In the end, guess what? I did it not nude, not eating a mini hot dog, not winking at the audience, not shooting Earth with my fingers. Movies are all compromise. Shit, I miss our fights! So these days when I go to these various conventions, signings at car dealerships or what have you, everyone asks (in girlish, teenage voice): 'Do you guys *still* talk?' (back to normal voice) We don't. But I plan to start a podcast to talk *all* about this stuff. People *need* to hear it."

DANI: "You both changed the world."

MAX: "Yeah. We did. We really did. '*I changed the world, ma!*' Goddamn!"

"All of Life is But a Spice Dream"

An Oral History of Terri Sparks's Final, Disastrous Photo Shoot

SPECIAL FOR THE 30TH ANNIVERSARY TIE-IN BOOK EDITION

Sarah Leopore, Los Angeles, 2023

In 2017, my partner and I invested in a property in the San Fernando Valley in Los Angeles: a modest 1950s tract house with all sorts of whimsical touches, such as a shake roof, gingerbread trim, wood-crafted built-in ashtrays still reeking of the lung darts of yesteryear, original "snapper sills"—windows designed to amputate the fingers of vagrants foolhardy enough to swipe a cooling pie. Just adorable, all of it. The house was intended to be a quick flip, and yet we fell in love (with ourselves and the house) while renovating and decided to move right in.

The previous owner, Clayton Sills, living in a retirement home, had worked decades as a commercial photographer, earning a small fortune specializing in, of all things, meat. He had an eye for, say, glowing up a ham or gravying over a brisket. His most famous photo for an advertisement had involved flowing silver silk curtains, a 1962 Bugatti roadster, a pre-fame, bare-chested Al Pacino, and a leaning tower of John Taylor's Sugar Cured Pork Rolls. The ad ran in the June 1965 issue of *Ladies' Home Journal.* The tag-line was "Pork Cures All!"

One day, not long after we moved in, I was tearing down a wall between the guest bedroom and a half-bath, when a dusty leather-bound album (tightly hidden between two embedded columns) fell to my feet. Opening the album (the cheap kind that one might find in any five and dime), I noticed there were dozens of 4 x 6 color photos of a woman I did not recognize. The previous owner's wife? His lover? Who *was* this? I showed it to my partner, Rhea. She, too, didn't recognize this … very distinctive-looking lady.

Neither did friends, associates, the new neighbors. No one seemed to know. But on a hunch, I took the album to a friend of a friend, lecturer and film historian, Jonathan Rosenfeld, at the UCLA School of Theater, Film and Television in Westwood. Perhaps this beautiful woman was, at one point in time, involved in showbiz? As it turns out, she *was.*

The sexy lass depicted in the photos, we were informed by Dr. Rosenfeld, was a little-known B-movie actress from the 1970s and 1980s named Terri Sparks. At the mention of the name, it dawned on me that I *had* seen Terri in a number of late-night cable movies from my childhood, with one in particular, *Toe People*, having left me quite shaken.

So we had established that it was Terri Sparks in the photos. And we had learned that Terri Sparks had been a working actress in mostly Drive-In and straight-to-cable movies. Fine. But what were photos of Terri doing inside an inexpensive photo album? And why was this album stored behind a wall? In *our* new house?

Intrigued, I set about asking the former owner, Clayton Sills, and others who knew Terri, about this very mysterious demoiselle's life … and about what turns out to have been her *final* photo shoot.

It wasn't for meat.

It was shot for—of all bizarre things—the sole purpose of helping Terri land a dream role in the 1994 cult movie *This Is How We Love.*

A role that, sadly, she never played. Hey, I never said this ended well, did I?

Terri and I never knew each other. We never met. We never talked. We never set eyes upon one another. And yet, and in a strange and mysterious way, I feel like we *did* know each other. I so very wish that Terri had been able to climb to the top of that Hollywood sign like she'd always dreamed—I'm talking metaphorically here—and not plunged downwards as she eventually ended up doing (and here I mean *literally*). As monuments to her legacy go, this very limited oral history will just have to suffice.

But hey, some of us don't even get *that*, right?

—SARAH LEOPORE *is the director of 2019's* Finally I Can Fly, *a Hulu three-part docuseries on Falcon Heene (aka "Balloon Boy"), as well as the author of the unofficial pictorial biography of legendary actor Randy Quaid,* God's Lonely Man *(Firestorm Press, 2021).*

JEM SCARBOROUGH, *film director.* Terri auditioned for me a number of times, and I cast her and she was always dynamic on the screen, but the roles she was best suited for in my opinion were not leading roles. Oddballs, carnies, petty thieves, night wanderers, unsuccessful whores. You get my drift. That was her milieu. And of course my pictures always reveled in that sort. I'll never forget the first time I met her, she was auditioning for me actually. My second picture: *Rail Jive Five.* About a clan of hoboes, trainhoppers who were high-end jewel thieves. I was looking to fill the role of "Railroad Bunk Whore," which sounds pretty seedy, and it was. Terri showed up and just blew us all away. Literally. She was an instinctual actress, and whip smart in her way. I hired her, sure, and I rewrote the part to honor Terri's intelligence and, let's say, experience. So this railroad whore character *knew* her history.

SOLLY HINCH, *former actress, Terri's frequent co-star.* I acted in a few pictures with Terri, yeah. There was *A Day Without Moonlight, Peacekeeper's Sexual Miracle, Grunt Squad Goes to Japan.* One thing about Terri, at least the times I worked with her, she hated learning lines. She'd rather make 'em up than commit 'em to memory. But she had her tricks. In *Grunt Squad* she wrote her lines on the front of all my wardrobe shirts, in big ol' three-inch letters. Course she made sure the wide shots had been done first; she'd just mumble in the takes, make shit up, but when it came time for her close-up, she'd always nail it, reading right off my front while talking to me. Remember when Rex Reed said she couldn't keep her eyes still and "had the focus of a hummingbird with Down Syndrome"? I ain't some kinda "woke joke" but I always wanted to slap Rex Reed for that. If you look closely when the camera's all tight, you can see her eyes moving back and forth as she reads her lines off my chest. That was a tell. Another was when her ears would burn red whenever she heard anything. Literally anything. Watch her ears in any movie. Whenever someone else talks, her ears burn red. She was crafty. I miss her.

PIPPY LARKIN, *President of the Terri Sparks Fan Club.* There's never been many of us, but we're committed. It's me, my cousin Ed Pace, and this woman from the library who refuses to tell us her name even though we've been meeting for close to ten years. I started the club because I was a huge fan of Terri in *Slum Detective* [1976]. When she took over the role, that franchise really popped. There was a feminine energy that cut through all that macho bullshit that was stuffed into those films, and it really spoke to me.

Then I watched everything I could get my hands on, close to three hundred films. There are only three titles our club can't find: *A Bottle of Rosé For Emily, Swamp Ruttin',* and *Why Can't We See Mike?* That's because they were made in Denmark and have weird content in them that U.S. law won't allow for. I get it, but I'd take an edited version! I mean come on! Edit out all that petting zoo stuff! Edit out all those sexy bits about falling in love with inanimate kitchen objects! Anyway, don't get me started on the U.S. government and Denmark, I could go all day. I hate them. I despise also Greenland.

JEM SCARBOROUGH, *film director.* Something most people don't know: Terri did a lot of stunt work. Whenever you see a woman getting her hair pulled in a movie between, say, 1968 and 1979? Chances are it's Terri. She did a brisk business in women's prison flicks. Grindhouse wig-whippers. TV Tuff Stuff. *Dukes of Hazzard.* Boss Hogg yanking Terri's hair. Or was it his basset hound? Lady got her mane yanked best. Don't know how she managed. Strong follicles. Episode of *Barney Miller,* the one when Fish grows a handlebar mustache and joins Scientology. Or maybe it was the Asian.

ANGELA JUGTREE, *Terri's childhood friend.* Terri and me talked on the phone a few times a week but this was back when it was expensive to call long distance so neither of us had the coins to talk long. Didn't help that when Terri did have coins she tended to whip 'em at homeless folks or buy BBQ Fried-Float-Ems. Last we spoke she was happy as a walrus and livin' it up at the Hollywood Stardust Motel. She had reached her pinochle.

LEVI TORKIN, *former manager of the Hollywood Stardust Motel.* When I came to work at Stardust, Terri was a long-time resident. Very long time. One of our "Last Stop Lassies" as we called 'em. Terri was the poster girl of Last Stop Lassies. Really. We built advertisements around her. "The Hollywood Stardust: Terri Sparks will likely die here!" Sides of bus jitneys, mostly. She loved 'em.

Yeah, I wanted Terri. We all did, all the men at the Stardust. Or so Terri told us. So she told a lot of fellas. No shame. She had love to spare.

BENNY GONZALEZ, *ex-lover.* I met Terri working in a banana ripening facility in Alhambra. Lotta people eat bananas every day, but ask them where their nearest banana ripening facility is, where bunches of green bananas get gassed with ethylene in temperature- and humidity-controlled rooms to push them to perfect ripeness for grocery store shelves? Well, most people have no fuckin' clue. That's sad.

[Mr. Gonzalez sits in silence, clenching and unclenching his fists]

Terri walked into the facility one day. Just off the street. Said, 'You guys hiring a banana handler? Because I've got bunches of experience!' Then she made a rude gesture and a clicking sound by kissing her front teeth. Woman off the street, feelin' sassy. The guys would shrug it off. But Anthony G.—his job was Chief Banana Handler—he took offense. Until he recognized Terri. He'd seen some flick she was in. Next thing you know, Terri's signing autographs. She signed almost every banana in the place. Quite a few plantains. And she was real pleasant, super chatty. Wasted, but in a way I found approachable. Spooking off downers. By the end of the shift me and Terri were an item. Or so she told me.

SOLLY HINCH, *former actress.* We were co-stars in *That Terrible Fire Make Wonderful Heat* [1975]. Played lesbian cavemen lovers in that one trying to escape a blimp inferno. And, well, we kinda had it going on on the side. Terri really liked to inhabit a role, so maybe it was all rehearsal to her. Either way, I didn't mind, she was a goddamn silk purse.

LEVI TORKIN, *former manager of the Hollywood Stardust Motel.* First time I set eyes on her I was working the front desk at the Hollywood Stardust. She told me to take a picture, it would last longer. Confused me. Then she listed a number of films she appeared in. I'd heard of some, not most. Garbage. Then she asked for a bathroom key. I wondered why she didn't use the head in her own room, and I told her so. And she snatched that bathroom key right from my fingers. I was in love. Or so she insisted from that day forward.

I can still see her now. Sashaying down the hall, bathroom key dragging and scraping behind her. We kept the key on a busted axle from an old AMC Gremlin. Long chain attached. Bad system.

I miss her! Or so she told me I would.

[Mr. Torkin pauses, then sighs]

Now I suppose you wanna talk about that photo shoot.

CLAYTON SILLS, *photographer of Terri's last photo shoot. [Editor's Note: Mr. Sills is 94 and suffers from dementia. He was accompanied by his home health aide Mary Graham Dot, who graciously volunteered to interpret Mr. Sills's more-difficult-to-understand statements.]*

Is this the ham salad?

MISS DOT: *No, Clayton. This young lady wants you to tell her about Terri Sparks.*

Who?

MISS DOT: *Terri Sparks. The actress? You remember taking her picture?*

I shot meat.

MISS DOT: *I know, Clayton, that was your specialty, but you also photographed people too. Do you remember?*

Is this the ham salad?

MISS DOT: *He does this when he's nervous. Clayton! See these photographs? You took them. You were once very successful!*

Is-is-is she meat?

MISS DOT: *No, that's a human, an actress. Terri Sparks is her name. You took photos. They found some photos in the walls of your old house.*

And in a boat at that! Can you imagine? (yelling) Hi Barbara! We're over here in the stable!

LEVI TORKIN, *former manager of the Hollywood Stardust Motel.* Terri was excited about this shoot. Like a bull elephant in a state of must. Said she was up for a role in an honest-to-god Oscar flick and these pics would seal the deal. Read about it in an issue of *Variety* she found lining her champion-pigeon cage. Would be for the astronaut's wife. Hired a lens-monkey fresh off a hot pork cured ad for something. Terri showed me the fella's work. I'll admit, he made those baloney flaps glisten. Terri said the trick was sprayin' 'em with chicken schmaltz. Used the same trick on Terri. Probably why her haunches have such a dewy look in the early shots. Not sure how that was supposed to help her land this rococo role, but there you have it.

SUSANNAH DALRYMPLE, *former assistant to producer James Calder Walton.* [Examines contact sheets] I've never seen these. [Puts them down] It's painful to look. I mean, the fashions of the time—so many ornamental grommets. But also, the circumstances were unfortunate. In the valley. Deep, deep in the valley. Where strangers fuck other strangers in rented warehouses made to look like suburban houses.

I might be responsible for this shoot happening. My boss, for like a week, was the producer on *This Is How We Love*. Total cretin. Just an . . . arrogant . . . how do I put this? Maryland hyena in DNA-crusted chinos. Invented that stuttering red doll. Or those stuffed dog toys. I can't remember. But he had a soft spot for Terri. Liked her in a few movies. Said she looked religious. Asked me to call Terri's agent and let him know that the director wanted Terri but was wavering. That was a lie. He just wanted to see her nearly nude. 'We love Terri but we want to see if she connects with this role.' Wanted to know, too, if she might modify her body if necessary up to and including budget Mexican cosmetic implants, that sort of thing.

Terri's agent [Benmont Waggers] was . . . very elderly. Difficult to communicate with. He apparently sold Newt Gingrich "challenge coins" and kept pushing me to buy some. Said they were lucky. And gas-station aphrodisiacs, years before it became a thing. Burro Power. Picture a donkey exploding upwards on a bottle rocket. That was one.

I did my best with the agent but something got lost in translation. The next day he called and said it was all taken care of, that he'd set up a photo shoot for Terri with some hot-shot deli meat photographer and it would "seal the deal" for *This Is How We Love*. Even said Terri would get calf implants by end of the week, which—we hadn't asked her to do that. But she did it anyway. On the cheap. Look close. You can tell. Like the legs of a fucking faun.

The whole thing was unnecessary. My boss just wanted to see Terri pose. He knew he wasn't going to hire her. But he liked her look. And he was a pervert.

BENNY GONZALEZ, *ex-lover*. Yeah, I recall the photo shoot. Terri and I were on again, off again by then. I knew there were other men in her life. Heck, there were other women in mine! I was a hotshot banana technician, living young and free in the greater Los Angeles area. You do the math!

What kills me is Terri was so excited about this particular shoot. This role [in *This Is How We Love*] was bigger than she was used to. She thought it could be a comeback type deal. Coming back to what, I don't know. Normally Terri didn't stress herself about things like "what to wear for an important event" or "whether or not to blow cigarette smoke in the face of an authority figure" or slipping on a pair of "non-imaginary underwear." But this was different. She spent double-figure minutes picking out an outfit. And she put on real underwear. We didn't have intimacy consultants back then, I can assure you.

SUSANNAH DALRYMPLE, *former assistant to producer James Calder Walton*. I was, pardon the expression, so nervous that I was floating out a befouled feather. The calf implants—my boss liked to be the one to pressure actors into getting those! I felt terrible! It was all for nothing anyway! So I slipped away to a pay phone on Melrose and called Terri Sparks directly. I knew she was living at the Stardust Motel. I'd seen the jitney ads. But when the guy at the front desk put me through to Terri's room, no one picked up. I was like, "Shit." This photo shoot, wherever it was happening, I knew I had to get over there and convince Terri it was a bad idea.

I don't totally remember how I got the address. I bribed someone at the Stardust with loose cigarettes and butterscotch NIPS. Turned out the shoot was happening over in Culver City in this huge warehouse. I rushed there. Inside, the smell was just atrocious. Lunch meat, pounds and pounds of it, sweating beneath French Fry Light-type lights. Stinkin' like the lower deck of Noah's Ark.

There was Terri Sparks, in the middle of it. Feeling no pain. I tried to get through to Terri but she was out of it. Reeked of chicken fat and fermented corn drink. And cinnamon whisk. Kept yelling at me, ordering me to yank her hair. I pulled her hair. Just a little. To appease her.

I told Terri the shoot was unnecessary. Told her she should put the bottle down, drink some water, and I'd help her tend to her suppurating calves. I tried everything to get her to listen. Nothing worked. In a way, I have to believe that nothing could have worked. Terri's destiny was set.

KEITH CAHANE, *former EMT.* I was an EMT in Hollywood in the 90s. Pure hell. I mean I don't regret it, but good God, all those movies about ambulance drivers in New York? Kitty cat go *whah whah*. I saw things that still make me weep on the sunniest of days. But life is good now. I'm the "Co-Head Chill-in-Charge" at the Margaritaville in Old Town Alexandria, Virginia. There are no bad days! Not because it's a Margaritaville, but because nothing can hold a cock-candle to the barnyard nights I experienced as a Hollywood EMT. Well, that and the bottomless plastic cups of Last Mangos in Paris!

As far as calls go, Terri's wasn't memorably awful. I mean, look, no death call is pleasant, but comparatively? Yeah, hers was more memorable for other reasons. When we first arrived, I truly thought the worst. Here was this airplane hangar-sized warehouse stacked to the rafters with different cuts of meat, parts made to look like a fancy suburban house. Before I knew anything, I thought for sure we'd stumbled on another Gacy, you know, some type of serial killer situation. But no, sadly.

SUSANNAH DALRYMPLE, *former assistant to producer James Calder Walton.* Lots of rumors about her death. Her breast implants didn't explode. Not sure where that came from.

BENNY GONZALEZ, *ex-lover.* She didn't overdose or poison herself with booze. She wasn't shot while skyjacking an Eastern Airlines jitney. Or die while lining coke off the Demi Moore pregnancy issue of *Vanity Fair.*

SUSANNAH DALRYMPLE, *former assistant to producer James Calder Walton.* Or prepping for a high colonic.

SOLLY HINCH, *former actress.* Or die while under anesthesia for the double calf implant. She never even went under anesthesia for the double calf implant! That was a double local.

ANGELA JUGTREE, *Terri's childhood friend.* Real simple. You want to know how she died? She died doing what she loved best. She was at her peak. She was auditioning for a major motion picture. Get it, not get it. It didn't matter. How could she have topped reading for a role in a movie produced by a Maryland businessman to play the alcoholic wife of an impotent astronaut fucking the Mexican gardener with a daughter married to a race car driver with half a face burned off? You can't. Massive heart attack. Forty-eight. Nothing. Just a kid.

KEITH CAHANE, *former EMT.* She looked real nice in the moment. Attractive even. You ever seen those sex dolls they show on the cable documentaries? The ones with the segments on swingers that always make the lifestyle seem more cringeworthy than appealing? But yeah, those sex dolls, real lifelike. That's what she reminded me of. Now I feel bad, comparing this dead woman to a sex doll. Look, the guy, the photographer was super nervous, just freaked out, and honestly probably coked up as well, who wasn't back then? But it was pretty clear he had nothing to do with it, she just put too many substances into her body over the years, too many dollar burgers, and she stopped cold, like a robot getting powered down. You know those sex robots in those futuristic movies?

We bagged and tagged her and took her straight to the morgue, sitting up in the back of the ambulance. I don't know if it was rigor mortis or what, but I just wanted to get her somewhere other than where I was. Her eyes were following me, least that's what it felt like. Like some sort of sexual painting in a sex museum just staring at you getting you all worked up for the sex. Pleading. You ever been to a sex museum? Check out the gift shop. Wild!

SOLLY HINCH, *former actress.* That's what the ambulance guy said? A natural death? For no reason? Nah. I think she was murdered. She knew too much, okay? She and Bill Clinton were a thing for a month. Took her out like he took out Vince Foster.

BENNY GONZALEZ, *ex-lover.* She said that? Vince Foster? Terri didn't even know who the hell Clinton was let alone Vince Foster! I believe she was involved with some deep-state shit. She was fucking an Israeli. So maybe she was a Mossad agent or something? Or an Iran agent? Lord, she did love the biscuit-skinned!

SUSANNAH DALRYMPLE, *former assistant to producer James Calder Walton.* I'm thinking Terri faked her own death. She's now living the good life somewhere special. I follow a person on Twitter named LovedMeSomeApples2. I'm thinking that's Terri. She absolutely adored apples. And she loved the number '2'.

KEITH CAHANE, *former EMT.* For fuck's sake, she died of a heart attack! Her veins were more clogged than Larry Flynt's cock.

SOLLY HINCH, *former actress.* Do I think about Terri? Well, hell yeah, I think about her all the time! God, what a waste! What she could have accomplished! In theory, any-way? Probably not much. But she was fun as blazes. Let's talk about me now: I run a large tech start-up. And I fly acrobatic jets for Red Bull on the side. Most weekends and nights. But if I'm not runnin' my billion dollar business or doin' air stunts in those jets, I'm thinkin' about Terri. And selling Herbalife to Catholic bitches in the suburbs.

JEM SCARBOROUGH, *film director.* I wish there were more actresses like Terri. I really do! Savvy, tough, hilari-ous, willing to work with me. Especially that.

PIPPY LARKIN, *President of the Terri Sparks Fan Club.* If I had to pick a favorite it'd probably be the first film of Terri's I ever saw, *Woman Eye Doctor III.* But there are a lot of runner ups! Like the Butter Boy trilogy for instance. People have asked me why I love Terri so much, considering most of the films she starred in were pretty low-budget and contain violent or depressing themes and images. I tell them that while Terri inhabited each of those characters with skill, what really shined was a woman committed to her craft, one that didn't give up, even when she was forced to spend an entire film in a filthy swamp playing a human catfish (*Pussygills*) or made to eat a six-foot-tuna-hoagie on camera in just one take (*Ravenous Philly Kim & The Flavor Squad*). She really inspired me to believe in myself and never, ever give up! I mean she was literally performing until the very end! Who cares if she was in a warehouse filled with rotting meat? She was doing what she loved! What a dream come true. Heaven.

Can't we just gaze upon the last shots of Terri Sparks and marinate in the beautiful wonder of it all? Can't we all just soak in the miraculousness of all that she accomplished, the millions of tiny little things that made so many countless people across the world so delirious with joy? And can't we just remember that she died doing what she loved most? Posing nearly nude for no money?

Can you pay me now?

Terri Sparks

The Disastrous Last Photo Shoot

JULY 8, 1991
11:30 AM – 4:30 PM

"I like to shower before I pose. It frees me up to be *dirty*."

"I'm *loving* this! Can we all come together in hot-joy vulval *unity*?"

"You don't like what you see? Then aloha on the steel guitar, sister!"

"Ever hear 'Going to Make You Sweat' by the M&M Music Factory?' Isn't it marvelous?"

"I yum this song. I wanna *scrump* it! Makes me wanna honk my *own damn* tiddies!"

"Sometimes when I pose I like thinking about a kid who lived on my block who could only talk by clucking. It grounds me."

"White Ace is my ace in the hole. The cider is cheap and ferocious, and I buy it by the brace. I also drink boxed wine! I call it my *cardboardeaux*."

"I like to dream jam off the giggle fruit!"

"There are rumors I slept with Mr Wendel from Arrested Development. Those are true."

"You break it, you bought it. All sales *final*."

"Can you *smell* that? That's hope."

"This is my *real* hair—pits, privates, piggies!"

"She's so dirty she's clean. That's how I *imagine* this character."

"I blow a kiss to the producer. Producer, catch kiss! *There are many more!*"

"I was born under a bad sign. It read: 'PLEASE NO LOITERING IN HOSPITAL PARKING LOT!'"

"It's called an 'Angel's Wink.' And it's *hereditary*."

"My one scar is tear-shaped. Find if you *dare*! Lower . . . (whispering) *lower* . . ."

"Do you like my blue-ish tinge? I take colloidal silver."

"In *Highland of the Great White North* I played an Eskimo lady who sleeps with an African. This is the face I made when making the romance!"

"Newhart taught me phone shtick. It's funnier when the phone is tiny. Here I am talking to God. I can also somersault backwards and talk in chimp."

"The Lord is funnier than people might ever know! My middle name is Nevaeh. That's heaven backwards. Am I stressed? No. Because that's *desserts* spelled backwards!"

"I was up for the teacher in Van Halen's 'Hot for Teacher.' They went with the *safer* choice."

"This ain't bragging: I can complete the *Soap Opera Digest* crossword in five minutes or less. With pen."

"Gail Sheehy's *Passages* is a major influence.
I'm packed with magic, mayhem and
mischief!"

"It's harmless. A physician's assistant in Korea
Town prescribed it."

"I've gone through men like a hot knife through fudge. I have childishly fresh eyes."

"Have you seen *Rhinestone*? I was up for Dolly's role. Didn't get it. *Politics*."

"Politics in that I have some very strong opinions about eugenics."

"I'm into fitness! Fit'niss Dexedrine in my mouth! Prayin' my prison dental work holds!"

"I'm a chanteuse who can coo a tune, a panther, pacing about, scratching my odorous mange against the bars of my cell! A product of some mad gods' deranged imagination! *Caged* heat!"

"I'm the queen bee, the nuts and *boiling* hot! Please check out my merch table!!!"

"I have fecal evidence that Big Foot is alive! I think it's Big Foot."

"My vagina is insured like a boxer's hands."

"Tuna. No crust."

"Sometimes when I need to reach the inner deep sad zone, I'll think about that monk who set himself on fire to protest the Vietnam War. Or scented candles."

"*I love you, papa!* That's from *Yentl*. I was up for the main role. *Politics*."

"Politics in that I have some very strong opinions about Judaism."

"Anyone want to take a peak into this old bird's rattled cage?"

"You smell that? *Lusti coconut oil*. Isn't it *divine*?"

"Shoot it! Right down *there*! In the *cookie zone*!"

"How about *this*?"

362

"I'll do whatever you want for this role! The *juice* is worth the *squeeze*!"

"My first and third husbands installed trampolines for a living. I'm single again!"

"I real freaky in the feathers!"

"*Papa, can I cook you a cheese blintze?* That's also from *Yentl*."

"You don't mind, do you? Not that I care."

"You! In the back! If you want some, find a stained coffee cup in the warehouse kitchen!"

"Husbands are like STDs. Everybody's has at least two! Just cause he's good for your hole don't mean he's good for yo *soul*!"

"I call these my Richie Rich boots! Touch them. *Higher.* Ain't they juicy?"

"I'm like Arthur. I does as I pleases! Do I
unease you?"

"*Whooooooo whooooooo*!!!!!!!!! I a runaway train
that churn on da *grape*!"

"You sure you don't want some, in the back? *Okay*! More for mommy!"

"You guys have a bucket? I did say no onions."

"Allow me to borrow your hat."

"Ready to go again! Sorry about your shoes!"

"I just 'went'. It's nature! And she has *summoned*!"

"This is fun! I once played a sexy gym teacher. She'd never flunk!"

"I'm-a *dance*!"

"Have you seen *Red Vaj of Courage*? I play a gardener."

"This is how you *do* it."

 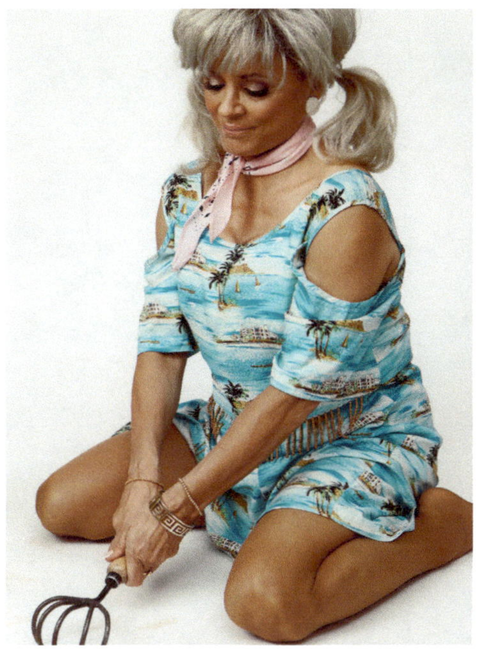

"And like *this*. This is how you *garden*. I can learn *anything*!"

"You put this into the ground and move your hands. You go, scrape, scrape, *scrape*!"

"You go, 'You want some water, flowers?! Here's some water from the hose, flowers!' That's how you *garden*!"

"Sprinkle, sprinkle, tinkle, *tinkle*!"

"'Hi! I'm the astronaut's wife! Welcome to our grand home! Would you like a drink? Here you go!' That's how I would do *that*!"

"'Welcome to our party at our *large* house! You don't have to take off your shoes! It's some pleasure to have you here in our *large* house!'"

"I know you from somewhere. Did you work on the set of *The Tourist Clap*? Wait! I remember! We both shop at ShopCheap Liquor! The one next to the methadone clinic! *Now* I ma-member!"

"A little woozy. But I'll push on! Can you validate this ticket?"

"All of life is but a spice dream!—uh oh—
mommy?! Is that you?! In the *cloud*?! I die now."

This Is How We Love:
The Official Posters

SOMETIMES THE EASIEST WAY TO LIVE . . .
IS TO DIE
This
Is How
We
Love
A SUNSHINE BEAM ENTERTAINMENT PRODUCTION IN ASSOCIATION WITH POOLESVILLE PRODUCTIONS
MAX PEARSON GLENN PRICE SHANNON FERGUSON ROBERT McGULLIGAN
RANDY SONDENFELD KERMAN GOTZ JENNIFER McMURPHY LEO CAPITALIANO
LANNY ADIL LUISA STENHENHET JOE ROSE COSTUME DESIGNER FREYA SELVEDGE
MUSIC BY LILL SONGERBERG CINEMATOGRAPHER PHIL CAMERON
PRODUCED BY JAMES CALDER WALTON WRITTEN & DIRECTED BY MATTHEW MICHAUD
RESTRICTED
UNDER 17 REQUIRES ACCOMPANYING
PARENT OR ADULT GUARDIAN

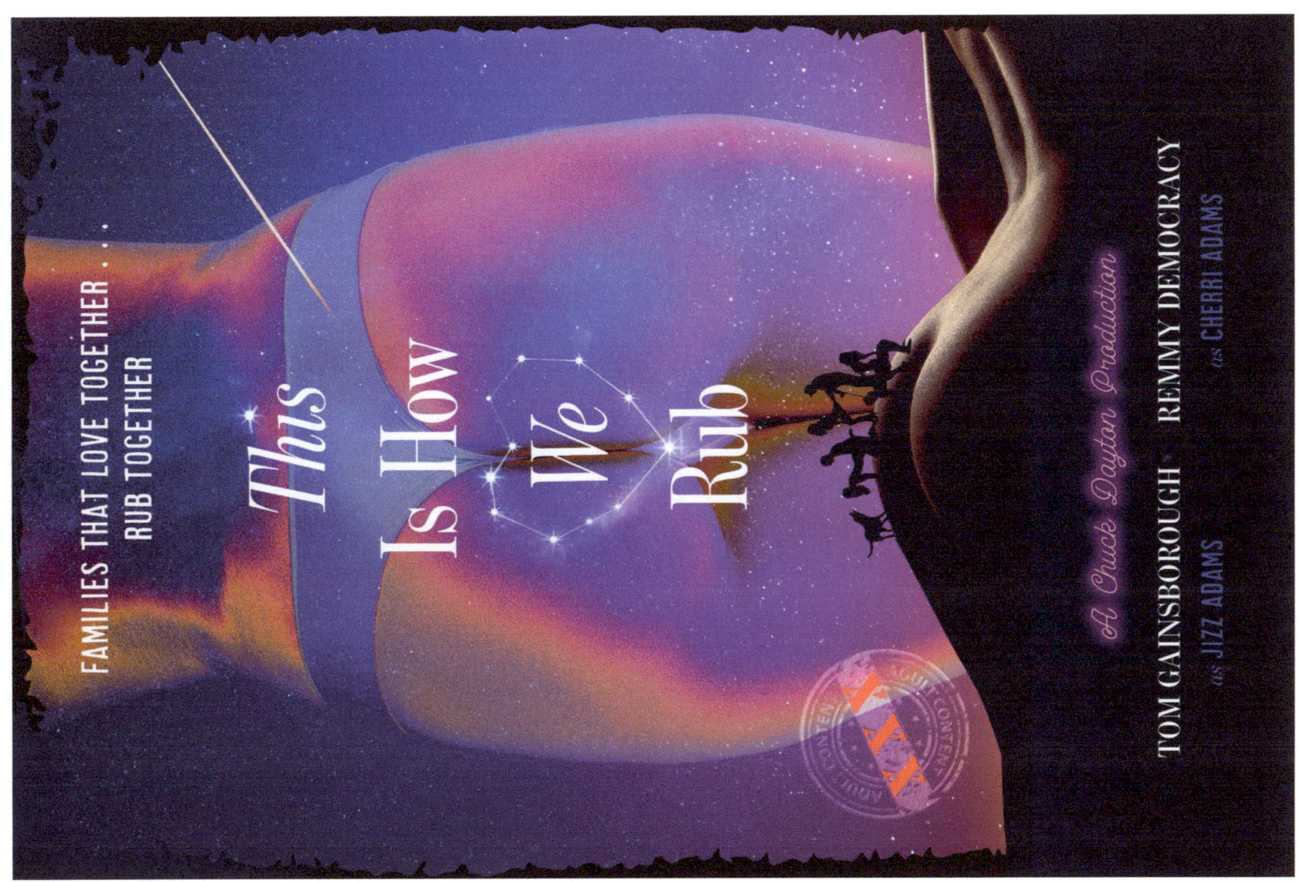

FAMILIES THAT LOVE TOGETHER ... RUB TOGETHER
This Is How We Rub
A Chuck Dayton Production
TOM GAINSBOROUGH
REMMY DEMOCRACY
as JIZZ ADAMS
as CHERRI ADAMS

LIKE THOUSANDS OF OTHER CINEMA LOVERS,

you adore wearing and enjoying a "pre-ripped" *This Is How We Love* T-shirt to impress strangers with admiration for a movie that has effected so many people in so many astonishing ways. And now you too can order your vert own *This Is How We Love* T-shirt in a great number of colors (raspberry, sunset, peacock, teal & lipstick), with a multitude of famous qoutes from the much adored film on the back! Fresh, alive, inspiring! Let's *do* this!

Model is wearing a size XS in style 01210SWT

A. "Give your former success my best!"
01210SWT. 50% Polyester /50% Cotton.

B. "You're a real tough woodchuck, huh?"
01211SWT. 50% Polyester /50% Cotton.

C. "I remember you! We formed an instant disconnection!"
01212SWT. 50% Polyester /50% Cotton.

D. "You oughta slack back, Jack!"
01213SWT. 50% Polyester /50% Cotton.

E. "Look at you two! Joined at the *un*hip!"
01214SWT. 50% Polyester /50% Cotton.

F. "You put the laugher in 'manslaughter'!"
01215SWT. 50% Polyester /50% Cotton.

G. "Once you go Persian, there ain't no other version!"
01216SWT. 50% Polyester /50% Cotton.

H. "Just because the deliveryman speaks Arab doesn't mean he's a *terrorist*!"
01217SWT. 50% Polyester /50% Cotton.

I. "Goddamn it all!"
01218SWT. 50% Polyester /50% Cotton.

As seen on ABC's Smash Hit "On Our Own"!

ORDER FORM ON BACK

ORDER FORM
UNISEX T-SHIRT

PHONE ORDERS CALL

301-299-7840

Make checks and money orders payable to:

EPIC / 15400 EDWARDS FERRY RD / POOLESVILLE, MD 20837

Please indicate method of payment:

- [ ] Check
- [ ] Money Order
- [ ] MC (16 Digits)
- [ ] VISA (13 or 16 Digits)

MasterCard VISA

EXP. DATE

CARD NUMBER

FIRST NAME ___________________

LAST NAME ___________________

ADDRESS ___________________

___________________ APT # ___________________

CITY ___________________

STATE ___________ ZIPCODE ___________

DAYTIME PHONE ( ) ___________________

SIGNATURE ___________________

	Style #	Color	XS	S	M	L	XL	Qty	Price	Total
A	01210SWT	O RASPBERRY								
		O SUNSET								
		O PEACOCK								
		O TEAL								
		O LIPSTICK								
B	01211SWT	O RASPBERRY								
		O SUNSET								
		O PEACOCK								
		O TEAL								
		O LIPSTICK								
C	01212SWT	O RASPBERRY								
		O SUNSET								
		O PEACOCK								
		O TEAL								
		O LIPSTICK								
D	01213SWT	O RASPBERRY								
		O SUNSET								
		O PEACOCK								
		O TEAL								
		O LIPSTICK								
E	01214SWT	O RASPBERRY								
		O SUNSET								
		O PEACOCK								
		O TEAL								
		O LIPSTICK								
F	01215SWT	O RASPBERRY								
		O SUNSET								
		O PEACOCK								
		O TEAL								
		O LIPSTICK								
G	01216SWT	O RASPBERRY								
		O SUNSET								
		O PEACOCK								
		O TEAL								
		O LIPSTICK								
H	01217SWT	O RASPBERRY								
		O SUNSET								
		O PEACOCK								
		O TEAL								
		O LIPSTICK								
I	01218SWT	O RASPBERRY								
		O SUNSET								
		O PEACOCK								
		O TEAL								

Shipping / Handling / Tax	
$00.00 Up to $10.00 . . . . . $2.75 $10.01 - $19.99 . . . . $3.75 $20.00 - $29.99 . . . . $4.75 $30.00 or more $5.75	
MD RESIDENTS ADD 5% SALES TAX	
U.S. Dollars Only	Total